I0653065

The Mormon Conspiracy:

A Flying Adventure

By

Dale M Seitzer

The Mormon Conspiracy

A Flying Adventure

Copyright 2009 Dale Seitzer. All rights reserved

ISBN 978-0-578-02795-1

Published by Seitview Publishing

A Flying Adventure

Dedicated to my father,

Lyle J. Seitzer

Chapter 1

40 Miles North of Pierre South Dakota

Jerry thought the guy just wanted a ride, what the hell is this? Now he was 2,000 feet above ground in a small plane headed North with a stranger pointing a gun at his ribs and he had enough.

"What do you want with me?" Jerry asked.

"Shut up!" the guy with the gun yelled with little bits of spit shooting out of his mouth.

"What is going to prevent you from killing me as soon as you are done with me? " Jerry demanded.

"Shut up and fly" he yelled louder still, while pushing the gun in his side. Jerry focused again on flying the plane but his mind was racing.

"You or your *associates* will kill me and my family as soon as we are not needed—I've seen plenty of movies and TV shows and they always end the same—the bad guy kills the hostage" Jerry was disgusted and frightened because the imminent danger of a gun in his ribs was impossible to ignore.

"SHUT UP" he yelled, even louder and fired a shot through the side window. The noise was shocking—it took Jerry's breath away, his ears were ringing in spite of the active noise reduction headsets and the roar from the engine and propeller. The smell of gunpowder burned his eyes and nose. The hot bullet melted the Lexan plastic window forming a perfect circle; the melted edges prevented the plastic window from cracking further. The gun had been pointed at Jerry's side:

the bullet must have missed his arm by inches.   Jerry did not like this guy with the gun—Jerry vowed that the guy will not succeed in whatever his mission was.   Staying in control and keeping a clear head would be a challenge but Jerry would need to do both. He must be alert and decisive to act when the opportunity arises.

Who is this guy?

Chapter 2

Pierre South Dakota Airport

his guy seemed normal – a plain looking guy – in his mid 30's. He looked common and nondescript, no accent, no unusual personality habits, disciplined enough to not allow anything personal to surface in their brief conversation. They met for the first time 2 hours ago- he was a friendly guy who just happened to be at the airport at the same time as Jerry, and just happened to be looking for a ride on a perfect flying day. He was interested in small planes and friendly. In retrospect it should have seemed weird that he asked all the 'right' questions.

He was "sort of" looking for a mentor to learn how to fly, and Jerry had been a mentor to new pilots. He also was interested in building a plane and Jerry built this plane, and he wanted to know where he could hook up with others with a similar interest. Jerry was a member and officer of the local Experimental Aircraft Association club at the airport. Too many coincidences.

The stranger was also very good at manipulation and Jerry would not know he had been manipulated until way too late.

The guy had not asked the typical newbie questions; How fast is this plane, how high can you fly, and is this dangerous? Instead, he asked questions that should have been a red flag. He asked about the gross weight capability of the ballistic parachute. He appeared to already know about the whole plane parachute

3

activated by pulling a handle to deploy a rocket which pulls the parachute out and inflates in 1.3 seconds. The ballistic recovery parachute then lowers the whole plane to the ground.

Then he asked about the empty weight of the plane and what was the shortest runway Jerry could land and take off from. Jerry should have known something was not as it seemed. When he asked these questions his eyes got narrower and his vocal tone was about half an octave lower. Then he would smile and say "This plane looks cool!"

He was about 6'1" and 180-190 lbs, mid 30's about 10 years younger than Jerry – he looked in good shape, well toned and he moved smoothly with no wasted energy. When Jerry shook his hand in greeting he felt plenty of calluses. No scars, no tattoos, the plainest clothes ever. He looked like a model for Mills Fleet Farm advertisements.

He wanted to see how the plane handled on short rough landing fields so Jerry suggested they go out to a little strip that was nothing more than an undulating field road. It was straight and there were no power lines so it was an easy in and out.

They got in the plane, Jerry on the left and he in the right seat, stowing a small leather soft bag under the seat. "Just a camera and stuff," he said.

"Why do you want to know how it handles short rough fields?" Jerry asked while tightening his seat belt.

"I have a place in the country and I want to fly from my own strip" he answered in a monotone voice.

"Yea, that's the dream of every pilot until you realize you gotta mow the grass every week." Jerry said with a laugh. The other guy didn't laugh; he just smiled and searched the horizon.

Jerry's plane was a Skyranger built from a kit. It looked like a typical small plane, propeller in front, wings above the cabin, tricycle gear -- 3 wheels with the steering done by the front wheel. It was constructed of steel and aluminum tubes covered in a Dacron fabric—it could carry two people but it was very light. It was bright yellow and white. The leading edge, ailerons and flaps were yellow and the rest of the wings and empennage was white.

Jerry reached for his lucky hat and sunglasses on top of the instrument panel. Jerry was a slim man with a strong jaw and tight skin and thin lips. He had an easy smile and a constant twinkle in his eye.

At 44 years old, he had a touch of grey and dark brown eyes and hair. He was self employed and independent. He was passionate about aviation and would talk to anyone at any time about anything aviation related. People who worked with him knew if they asked about airplanes they would receive a long thoughtful discussion.

Jerry led him through a complete preflight inspection and walked around the plane pointing out the plane's features. They warmed up the engine, made their radio calls and departed the airport. Jerry was proud of the plane and its performance so he pulled the nose high and climbed out at a steep angle meant to impress the passenger. The plane had a ground roll of about 100 feet and climbed at 1200 feet per minute. Jerry smiled and looked over at the passenger and did not receive any kind of connection.

They turned away from the airport in a gentle banked turn and headed north to the landing strip. It was a wonderful spring morning; the grass was green and just a hint of green in the fields. Clear visibility—they would be able see for 20- 30 miles in the South Dakota prairie. Very light winds now and light winds predicted all weekend.

Jerry looked over at his passenger after he checked the engine instruments. He did not look like a guy on his first airplane ride – he was scanning the instruments, looking at the wings and landing gear and spending several seconds on each engine and flight instrument as if he knew exactly what they were for.

The landscape around Pierre is breathtaking – there is a big river with wildlife and clear blue water. Rolling hills covered in green are everywhere, huge chunks of woods near and along the river break up the prairie fields. Sunrises and sunsets are glorious any time of year. On this early morning flight the shadows from the rolling landscape made beautiful patterns on the ground.

Jerry continued the climb and turned north towards the private strip. He pointed out landmarks and wildlife when he could see them. Jerry's passenger wasn't much for conversation—Jerry understood that—sometimes he likes to just be quiet and enjoy the scenery.

"Hey" he said with a little laugh, "I forgot to ask your name, I'm Jerry, what's yours?"

"Joe" he said succinctly.

Jerry then asked, "Are you a hunter?"

"Why?" he quickly asked—eyes widening with surprise.

"Oh it seems like everyone in South Dakota is a hunter. Not for me though—good days for hunting are also a good days for flying," Jerry said, trying to be entertaining. He added with a smile, "Just about everybody in South Dakota hunts something."

There is no secret to flying an airplane. Pilots all use checklists so they do not forget any items. Every switch and gauge in the cockpits is labeled with minimum and maximum readings indicated. Jerry read an article about a couple of good old boys who stole a plane and took it for a joy ride. They explained that even though they never flew before, they just followed the instructions on the checklists. Jerry stowed his check list where it would be easy to grab.

A Flying Adventure

Jerry quickly found the landing strip just 17 miles from the airport. He flew at 500 feet above the ground against the wind over the strip to check for obstructions. Then a left hand turn at the end of the runway and another left hand 90 degree turn – now they were downwind. This is the pattern for landing and puts the plane in position for a standard approach. The idea is that each landing would be very similar, reduce power at the same point each time, the same location in relationship to the runway—every time. In this case, a short and rough field, just dirt and grass, so Jerry would slow the approach speed as much as possible and dive to the runway rounding out right above the runway. Hold the plane off the ground, without touching down and delay landing until the plane has reached its slowest speed.

Slow landing speed puts the least amount of forces on the landing gear and is an important factor in a short field landing. The grass strip is too short for bigger faster planes but Jerry's plane could land easily in about half the runway distance.

They stop because Joe wants to look the plane over and check the landing strip.

"Well, what do you think?" Jerry asked trying to be cheery.

"Yea, fine" was all he said. That's when Jerry first asked under his breath,"Who is this guy?"

Joe pulls out his phone to check reception and announces he has no service and asks if he could borrow Jerry's. Jerry thought it was odd – there are cell towers everywhere.

"What kind of phone do you have?"

"Verison" he said while trying to hide the phone from Jerry. His phone did not look like any phone Jerry had ever seen—it was thicker with a short thick antenna—maybe a satellite phone

"I have T-mobile and it works pretty well—maybe your phone is broken - let me look at it." Jerry offered.

"No" Joe quickly said, and shoved the phone into his bag. "Could I borrow your phone for a short call? I want to tell my buddy about this great plane of yours," smiling for the first time in over an hour. Jerry handed over his phone.

Joe quickly dialed a number and began talking and walking to the other side of the plane. He finished the call and returned to the same side of the plane as Jerry was checking the landing gear. Jerry was on one knee looking at the tire and wheel when he looked up to see a gun pointed at him. Joe's face was chilly like a granite rock; he stood confident—close enough to minimize the chance of missing but far enough away so Jerry could not reach him in any defensive maneuver. The gun was big and camouflaged colored. Jerry knew very little about guns --- it looked very sleek and modern handgun. While he was aiming his gun at Jerry he slipped his phone in his pocket. Jerry's face was flush with embarrassment and fear.

"What? Are you stealing my plane?" Jerry asked sounding like a smart ass. His wife always poked him in the ribs when he said stuff like that. His assertiveness embarrassed her. 'Just give him what he wants.' she would say.

Jerry's mind was racing trying to understand what was happening—"Is this joke?" He asked as he stood up.

"Shut up or I'll shut you up!" Joe said hitting him in the gut. Jerry fell to his knees and could not breathe. Joe wondered if Jerry would just give up or if he could be forced to complete the task.

Jerry would have gladly given him the plane,
"Here take it, the plane," no response from the guy with the gun.
"Not a problem, it's full of fuel, I'll just walk to a farm house," he said waving his hand. Still no response.

"Probably take me a couple hours to find a ride—you could go a long way in a couple of hours"

"Shut up, and do what I say," Joe sneered.
He got his fancy phone out, made a call while pacing around Jerry on the ground. They were at least 5 miles from any civilization surrounded by corn and wheat fields. There was nowhere to run, no one would hear him yell; even a gunshot would be ignored – everyone would simply figure someone was doing a little hunting. Jerry could try to defend himself but was no fighter. Jerry had no choice but to go along and wait for an opportunity.

Chapter 3

65 Miles North of Pierre, South Dakota

A cool breeze came through the bullet hole in the side door, the gun was still pointed at Jerry's side and he could still smell the gun smoke. A fun Saturday morning demonstration flight has turned into a kidnapping. Now he was flying north concentrating on controlling the plane while analyzing the situation. This was clearly an emergency but not one Jerry felt prepared to handle.

The basic pilot mantra for an unusual situation is FLY THE PLANE. He decided to stay as calm as possible and gather more information.

"Hey, Dude," Jerry said, "where is the safety on that gun of yours?"

He just stared at him and said "Shut up"

"Look, you cannot wave that gun around with out the safety on so please put on the safety" Jerry might need to use that gun and he wanted to know how the safety worked.

"I am the pilot in command so do what I say!" Joe held up the gun and petulantly flicked the lever with his thumb.

"Thank you" Jerry said sarcastically.

Joe controlling his anger at Jerry and slowly said, "Shut up." He thought about the price Jerry would pay even though he had not chosen to participate. The project is bigger than any one person, sacrifices must be made—total commitment is required.

They were flying at about 2,000 feet above the ground at about 95 mph. They were about an hour from Pierre and about 2 more hours before they would need more fuel. Jerry knew he would be stiff and tired long before the fuel stop. Small planes are not known for their luxury and comfort.

Joe was at least 10 years younger than Jerry and has the stamina and focus of youth.

"What's your plan? Where are we going? Why are we going? Why do you need me?" Jerry asked a series of questions trying to find a way out.

"Shut up, you don't need to know" Joe said as he shifted his grip on the pistol.

Joe pulled out an odd looking handheld device that looked like it could be a GPS unit—but like nothing Jerry had ever seen before—it looked more industrial or military. It was small and thin and had a large color moving map. He said "Make a heading of 349.7."

That is almost due north – Jerry adjusted his portable Garmin GPS in the instrument panel to line up with the suggested heading. Jerry looked at his Sectional map for airports or military operating areas along the way—maybe he could get intercepted by a military plane and be rescued, but what would happen to his wife and kids?

Jerry snuck a peak at Joe; this guy was much more than he seemed. Was he ex- black operations? Some kind of secret spy? A foreign agent? It seemed like he had a lot of backing but what can he do to survive? Jerry thought, who was he working for? Maybe he is a free agent or a lone wolf. Who else was in on this, how big is this operation? What was he going to have to do to get of this alive?

Chapter 4

South Dakota

On the ground on an uncharted landing strip 17 miles north of Pierre South Dakota, earlier the same day, the intense man with the gun shoved his phone in Jerry's face, "Here, talk." He demanded.

"Hello? Jerry, Honey, is that you?" a faint nervous female voice is heard.

"Yea, Lynn, what's happening?" Lynn and Jerry were married 14 years ago and have 10 and 12 year old girls. Lynn said, "There are guys here in our house with guns—are you in trouble?" as she held the hand of her youngest daughter.

"It looks like trouble has found us..." Jerry said as the man with the gun grabs the phone and yells in it, "Shut up"

"OK, asshole, we have you, and your family. I don't care about any of you, I am already dead so don't think of trying anything. You're gonna do what we say and your family will live. If you do anything stupid they die and you suffer." The last 3 words were said very slowly.

"What is this all about?" Jerry interjected while straightening his shirt and pants.

"This is not a discussion—shut up and listen!" He slammed Jerry in the stomach again and Jerry collapsed to the ground again, gasping for air.

Jerry was seething between clenched teeth, "I'm going to give him everything he gives me – I hate this guy." Lucky for Jerry, Joe did not hear.

"Get in the plane now and let's go" he said in a softer tone as he searched the horizon. Jerry struggled to his feet and folded himself into the plane. Screw the preflight, let's just get out of here and get this done—what ever *this* is, Jerry thought. Is this a situation where he should crash the plane killing them both in order to stop the mission? His first priority was to escape and rescue his family but he was ready to kill this bastard and die himself to stop these people.

Joe checked his list carefully shielding it from the pilot – they are right on track. Everything was going perfectly.

Jerry taxied back to the other end of the rough dirt strip and watched the engine temperatures rise up to normal operating levels. He put in one notch of flaps because of the short rough strip—he needed to get off the ground quickly and avoid damage to the landing gear of this light plane. Use of flaps allows more lift for short field take offs and allow a slower descending and landing speed.

The Rotax 912S, 100 horse power engine cranked up with full throttle, the nose wheel lifted off the ground and the main wheels were off the ground a couple of seconds later. Jerry pushed the stick forward and the nose lowered to continue flying close to the ground so they could increase speed and then start the regular climb. Around the airport Jerry was the guy all the other pilots say, 'Jerry knows how to fly that plane – he can get into and out of any landing strip.' Joe had done his research – Jerry was actually carefully researched and selected not just picked at random.

An airplane doesn't care what it is carrying. It just runs. Planes are just machines that will run or stop regardless of the importance of the operation. It just seems like machines fail when we need them most. Jerry was hoping the engine would sputter and stop, but no, it just hummed along toward an outcome that neither of them could foresee.

Jerry did not know what would happen to him if the plane failed—would he be shot after they landed or would Joe let him go? Jerry figured this plane was selected because it had a ballistic recovery parachute – it could prevent the pilot from intentionally crashing the plane. If the engine started to run rough so the mission would be delayed, he might need to find someone else to kidnap—but the engine just runs.

Normally a pilot wants the engine to stay running but now Jerry was hoping for a sputter. Joe, on the other hand, wanted the engine to just keep humming. He watched the instruments, monitored the engine, and listened to the drone of the propeller aware of every change.

Chapter 5

Pierre, South Dakota

I t could have been a great flying day, high clear skies, moderate winds and no chores at home. The landscape was absolutely beautiful, different shades of spring green alternating with the different brown tones of earth. The delicate shade of green from new leaves and shoots fades and glows with the shadows of the early morning sun. The clay and sandy areas and the gullies leading to the creeks which lead to small rivers and between the gullies, flat fields of corn, soybeans, wheat and grass and alfalfa mixed reminded him of quilts his mother and grandmother's had made.

On the Great Prairies you can see for miles—not a lot of trees and pretty flat. Some pilots dream of mountain flying—but Jerry just likes to get up and out. The Dakotas are not heavily populated but from the air one can see numerous small towns, roads, railroad lines and the ubiquitous cell phone towers. From the air a pilot can see how the landscape fits together. Creeks run to streams, streams flow into rivers. Railroads connect cities and towns—one about every 10 miles or so. Many roads are laid out north / south and east / west in an evenly spaced grid with a road generally every mile or so. Every 10 miles or so there will be a larger paved road. The farther north they go there will be less civilization but really they would never out of sight of someone on the ground until the northern edge of North Dakota.

Flying a plane requires full concentration but it is a good activity when you need a break from daily stress. A pilot's senses are occupied from the minute they step into the hangar. There is a rote practices ritual to prepare to fly. Reviewing the items on a preflight checklist puts the pilot in the correct frame of mind. There is a great sense of accomplishment from learning to fly and flying is a good discipline.

Pilots plan for emergencies, understand and plan for risk. Life is a constant calculation of risk and cost and value. They want the reward of having fun and work to minimize risk involved in flying but ultimately they understand every activity carries some risk.

What is the risk calculation for a fanatic pointing a gun at the pilot in a small plane? This is way off of Jerry's risk chart.

Jerry tells people he likes flying because there are long periods where you just look at the scenery and are alone with your thoughts. He is not uncomfortable being alone for long periods. His wife, Lynn is a pilot too or maybe it should be Lynn is a pilot and Jerry is a pilot too.

She earned her pilots wings before Jerry - they support each others interest in aviation. Either way the message is the same- flying is a fun family activity.

Lynn kind of sings when she talks—her voice has a natural pitch variation that sounds like a song bird—even when she makes the simplest request. 'Honey, can you get some kitty litter too?' An unintended result is that even when she is making small talk, to Jerry it sounds like she is speaking the dialog from a pornographic movie. His buddies don't hear her like he does—that's why it is called love. He just smiles a sly wry smile when he thinks of the fun times he has with Lynne.

She is thin, but not skinny, long brown and red hair (usually in a Pony tail) a big smile and soft skin. She is an active woman who likes to keep busy. She thinks she is a great singer –

especially country music. Jerry never complains – he always smiles and says, 'That's great honey! Sing some more.'

He looked at the kids as they played in the yard and smiled. "I'm a lucky guy."

Jerry describes his kids as the coolest little humans anywhere. It seems like they each got the best traits of their Mom and Dad. They have the longest eyelashes around the biggest, brightest eyes; people say they have 'smiling eyes'.

He wants to see them be defiant teenagers; he wants to be there to see them embarrassed by what their parents say and what they wear. Lynn is the more protective parent. Jerry wants them to experience life and all the risks. He doesn't push them into risky activities but when they were younger he taught them how to cross the street and then gave them permission to explore. Lynn wanted them to stay on the block.

They expect them to wear a helmet when they rode their bikes or skateboards and Jerry always wears a helmet when he rides his motorcycle. Consider the risk, plan to reduce risk, but get out there and enjoy life, it was a family philosophy.

Lynn had woken up late on this Saturday morning– she knew Jerry would be flying early. He would call later to let her know when it would be her turn. Flying had seemed like a good activity they could do together. Right now with the kids, doing anything together required a lot of planning so they took turns. Jerry would get back to watch the kids while she has a chance to fly too.

One of Jerry's first flight instructors suggested practicing specific skills every time you fly. As Jerry drove out to the airport he had thought, 'I wonder what I should practice today.' Lynn needed to prepare for her biennial flight review. Every 2 years pilots must fly with a certified flight instructor and get

17

checked out.   Flying is somewhat like golf. One can always get better and it takes regular practice AND practice is fun. Jerry had just completed his flight review; maybe today would be just for fun.

Chapter 6

Sherwood Residence Pierre, South Dakota

The kids were still in their bedrooms when she heard the back door open. She figured it was Jerry when she said, "Jerry is that you? What are you doing home?" She turned the corner and saw 5 big guys with masks stream into the kitchen and then fan out through the house. She yelled and screamed and kicked but they immediately had handcuffs, a blindfold and gag on her. Before the blindfolds went on, she saw big men wearing dark utility outfits with guns, knives, armor, helmets and masks. She heard the girls moan as they were pushed onto the couch next to her. They were all shocked and scared silent.

So far there had been no talking out loud, just whispers as the doors were locked, the window curtains drawn, security system disengaged and the phone unhooked. The men were using some sort of wireless communication between themselves and with someone else. No wasted motion—like a well rehearsed play. What was going on — were they police or Army or some sort of spy? Now that the adrenaline was wearing down, she felt angry – how dare they come in here and push us around. She worked to remove the gag and then tried to stand up. She was firmly pushed down

"What do you want? Get out of my house! If you hurt these kids, you will pay!" Just as she got the last word out-- the gag was put back on and she was pushed down by firm hands.

19

More hushed speaking and heavy foot steps, then some different footsteps. She was jerked to her feet, someone shoved a phone to her ear and she heard a voice say, "Say hello to your husband."

Jerry sounded very distant—he did not know what was happening. He said hello in a slow uncertain drawl. She knew instinctively this was not a random act – this was a definite conspiracy. She knew she was in the middle of a well designed, organized and well equipped operation for some unknown purpose. She did not like to be ignored so she kept asking "What? Why? And who?"

After what seemed like almost an hour, Lynn and the girls, still in their pajamas, were herded to an upstairs bedroom and boards were screwed into the outside of the door and door jamb. Inside they removed each others gags and blindfolds. A quick review of the kids showed they were healthy but scared. There was a bathroom off the bedroom and they could talk. She did not notice the portable audio and video camera in the corner of the room near the ceiling by the door. They were trapped—a jump from the windows would result in some injuries. She could probably make it but leaving the kids was not an option. Sending one of the children would be way too risky. Lynn's car was moved out of the garage and the intruder's vehicles must have been moved into the garage. The men were really well organized but no one could think of everything – she decided to just watch and listen and plan to be ready when any chance came.

The questions from the kids were the same questions Lynn had, "Who are these people, Why us, why now? What next?" She comforted the kids and put a smile on their faces by saying, "Everything will turn out fine – don't worry"

Chapter 7

Pollock, South Dakota

"What are you? Some kind of terrorist? What is your cause? Who do you work for? Why are you doing this? What are you doing? Why me?" The guy turned in his seat so he could see Jerry with both eyes and he just stared. After a pause he said, "This is the last time I will tell you. Shut UP!"

His tack is not working—Jerry could not intimidate him, he could not manipulate him, he could not fight him, but Joe needs Jerry. He needs something only Jerry can provide. Joe doesn't have a heart filled with rage—he controls his emotions but there is anger buried beneath the surface. He is very goal oriented and he is a planner. Joe must have had some flight training because he is so comfortable in the plane. He looks at the plane like he knows what he is looking at. Jerry thinks he had some military training the way he handles the gun, the way he can fight and plan and how he moves with a captive. The way he can control himself, how he can blend in and get people to do what he wants, makes Jerry think he has a lot of undercover training and experience.

Then Joe really surprised Jerry—he pulls out a checklist of things to do. Jerry read a few items—a list of equipment: GPS, satellite phone, gun, ammunition, knife, taser, pepper spray and map and then a list of numbers.

He hit Jerry with the gun in his forehead when he sees Jerry sneaking a peek at the check list. Jerry sees stars and as he jerks around, the plane flops in the air. A steep bank to the right and then a steep bank to the left as Jerry opened his eyes and tried to get control of the plane again. Joe's bag gets spilled on the floor of the plane and he yells

"Hey, jerk' fly the plane." Joe said as he replaced the gun in Jerry's side.

This is a very small plane – there is no auto pilot – the pilot needs to fly the plane and keep it pointed in the right direction at all times. Joe rubs his head where it hit a structural tube over the top of the cabin. Jerry is shorter than Joe and inches away from the cross tube but with the temporary loss of control and wild maneuvering, Joe receive a knot on his head. Jerry smirks to himself when he sees the lump form on Joe's head.

They loose 400 feet of altitude and Jerry accidentally grabbed the throttle and pulled it to idle. The airspeed had dropped to dangerous levels but Jerry worked to get the plane under control and stabilized. Blood was flowing into one eye so now Jerry was flying with only the other eye. He had a larger challenge—controlling his anger at this idiot with the gun.

Jerry did not see first aid kit on Joe's check list but he supplied a large bandage and reached up and placed it over the gash in Jerry's forehead. The guy with the gun almost looked like he was showing empathy.

He needed to change tactics and the door was open. Jerry wiped out the blood from his eye.

"Thanks a lot for the bandage – I can't count how many times you told me to shut up. I apologize for ignoring you." Jerry said repentantly.

A Flying Adventure

"Fly the plane" he said calmly. He studied what must have been a GPS unit and says,

"We are a bit off course, and we need a heading of 357" Jerry turns the plane a bit and lines up between 35 and 36 on the GPS compass.

After a couple of minutes Jerry said with fake respect, "You look real comfortable in the air—are you a pilot?" No response.

"Do you want to fly the plane a while?"

He was quiet – thinking about the offer—"Just fly the plane," he said softly and he turned to look out the window. Joe was getting distracted by the pilot – what a doofuss – he thinks he can develop a relationship with me. He is so naïve.

A small herd of deer run together near a kidney shaped slough and Jerry points, "Hey look at that herd of deer – look at them run" he said. Joe looks out the window and actually smiles a little. The deer herd zig- zag a little and dart into a thick field line of small trees and large bushes. These field lines are planted to reduce soil erosion from the wind. Deer are abundant because they have plenty of food and few predators.

"What is happening with my wife and daughters?" Jerry asked slowly and calmly while trying to sneak another peak at his reactions.

After a pause Joe said steadily, "Your family will be fine if you do what I tell you. If you screw up, they die. The man in charge of that operation is very efficient and loyal. They are safe for now but I can't protect them forever. If there are any problems, his instructions are clear"

"So, if I help, they get killed and if I don't, they get killed," Jerry said not expecting an answer. Both men had faces of disgust for different reasons.

Chapter 8

3 miles South East of Mc Clusky, North Dakota

T he satellite phone started ringing – a weird haunting ring that sounded like some science fiction sound effect. Joe tried to answer the call but with all the noise in the cockpit—the guy with the gun cannot hear. There is no way to hook the headset to this phone. He said, "Land now, I need to take this call."

"There is an airport 7 miles ahead—we will be there in about 5 minutes." Jerry said thinking maybe this would be an opportunity to escape.

"No, I mean land now! Right there!" he insisted. Jerry looked down and saw a large pasture with no cattle. Joe lifted the gun into Jerry's line of sight and said simply,

"Land there. NOW!"

Jerry switched to emergency landing mode—he chopped the throttle to idle, and cranked in a tight descending spiral down. After 2 and a half turns at 500 feet above the ground, he put in full flaps and leveled out into the wind. Normally one would fly over the landing area to check for rocks, fences, and ditches – this time they will have to land and use up some of their good luck.

There is a saying that every new pilot is given a bunch of good luck when they start flying. As they learn they use up that good luck to overcome mistakes and poor judgment while they gain experience and skills. The goal of the pilot is to learn how to fly safely before they use up their good luck.

The field wasn't exactly flat, there were little hills and valleys; Jerry climbed with the little hill and descended on the other side. The wheels touched on the next uphill and rolled to a stop in knee high dry grass. Jerry could hear the tall grass getting trimmed by the spinning prop. He turned off the engine by turning off the magnetos. The whole landing took about 90 seconds from decision point to engine off. Joe had a look of respect for the pilot – they selected the right man for this job.

He exited the plane and stood in front of the plane and talked in quick staccato sentences—both he and Jerry were anxious. He held up his hand instructing Jerry to stay in the plane. Jerry looked around the cabin, checked the fuel level and took another peek in Joe's bag—no weapons. After about 45 seconds he got back in and said,

"Let's go."

Jerry started the plane, turned around and taxied to the top of the hill. The pasture was quite bumpy so slow taxi speeds were needed, Joe impatiently said,

"Let's go!"

"Cool your jets, Romeo" Jerry barked. "Look at how bumpy this pasture is, Trust me," said Jerry with a smarmy smile. They took off into the wind starting with a little down hill run. The plane got off the ground in a normal short - rough field take off and continued climbing while correcting to the desired heading.

"We are going to need fuel soon," Jerry said. "Any one of these airports will have fuel and be open right now" he said holding up the map and pointing to their location.

"No, go to these coordinates 101.54.09 -- 45.28.45. We already have a private strip lined up with fuel." He said confidently.   Jerry entered the coordinates into his GPS and adjusted to get on course to the landing area.

"Canada" Jerry said out loud.   His butt was sore, he had to go to the bathroom, and he was thirsty and ready for a break.

Jerry calculated they had enough fuel left, the plane was working well and the engine was running as smooth as ever. He was trying to figure out a way to get a message to the police or anyone for help. Maybe he could sabotage the plane to make it run poorly, but he has had no chance to get under the cowling.

Joe was also thinking, planning like a chess match – two three and four steps ahead, planning for every alternative.   His training prepared him to deal with impossible missions. He made a commitment to this cause; he pledged his life and promised to do what ever it took to complete the mission.

*   *   *   *

Every plane has a transponder which sends out a signal to airport radar stations with identifying information, speed and altitude.   There is a special code to airport personnel -- 7500 on the transponder will tell the air traffic controllers the plane is being hijacked.   Normally it is set on 1200. Up to this point the guy with the gun has kept the transponder off.   At the next opportunity Jerry will turn the transponder on and set it for 7500 to signal the air traffic controllers the plane has been hijacked.

This might work but Jerry was in the middle of North Dakota and headed north—hundreds of miles away from an airport with air traffic controllers. Perhaps another plane will pick up the signal and pass the word on. This was a long shot and if caught there would be much more serious consequences.

The terrain has changed from rolling wheat fields to more rugged - less fertile land.   In the distance they saw dozens of small lakes.   They were just a few miles from the refueling spot. The GPS unit indicated the landing area was just ahead.

A Flying Adventure

As usual Jerry flew over the strip at about 1,000 feet above the ground; he checked the wind sock, looked to see how flat the runway was, the condition and length. As he flew over, he saw black Chevy Suburbans. One at each end of the runway and one parked off the runway about halfway down. This strip was in the middle of no where – no houses or farms for miles around, those trucks had to drive almost a mile to the nearest gravel road. The strip was not on the sectional map—not really a surprise, there were plenty of private strips that were not on the maps. Normally one would need an emergency situation or permission to land at an indicated private landing strip. Jerry had a guy with a gun pointed at his side – that would count as an emergency.

Jerry turned left at the end of the runway, turned left again, went down wind and then left again lined up for landing. On final, the turn that puts the runway in the windshield, he slowed to 60 miles per hour, put in the full flaps and reduced the throttle to idle. The plane settled in on the narrow smooth turf runway.

The people near the black SUV's were wearing dark grey utility suits, body armor and carried hand guns, knives, radios and assault rifles with big ammo clips. Two people at each vehicle –when they got closer they could see they wore some kind of helmet and a face mask—who were these guys?

Joe recognized a couple of the guys by the way they wore their body armor and held their weapons. He had been on missions with them in Afghanistan. They were all team oriented and followed orders without question.

Jerry swiveled his head watching Joe and the guards, trying to see when he could make the change to the transponder to let someone, anyone, know he was hijacked.

The guy with the gun said, "Taxi up to the middle of the runway and stop there." He turned to Jerry and continued, "See all those guys with the masks and guns," pointing to the well armored big guys. "They do not have the sense of humor I have."

"Their lives will be easier if you are dead, so don't do anything stupid." Joe looked at Jerry to see if he has any self confidence – if he was confident he may do something rash. Joe needed him to be scared, nervous and focused on flying.

Jerry needed to pee so he shut the engine down and unhooked his seat belt, got out and stretched his legs. One man had a gas can and began pouring the fuel in the gas tank. There is no talking between the guys on the ground—they know what to do and work like a single unit. The guy with the gun brought sandwiches and drinks for them.

Jerry verified fuel used – they were using almost four and a half gallons per hour – that was right on the expectation. Jerry paid close attention to fuel consumption and quality—they do not want to run out of gas in the air.

After Jerry had a chance to do a post flight inspection he started to take some glances at these guys—they were all large – tall men. This was such a well prepared operation—none of this was a coincidence. Everything was well planned—where they go, when they stop, who does what. No comments between the guys, no yelling, no instructions—it seemed like there was someone above them all that was directing everyone.

Joe talked briefly and privately with the other guy dressed in black. "Any problems?" he asked.

Joe said quietly, "No problems at all, good job planning – he is a whimp, nothing to worry about here."

"Have you gotten any reports from the others?" Joe asked.

"Nope, not a peep – they never tell us grunts what is happening anyway," he said with a chuckle. His partner got another can of gas, emptied it into the plane's fuel tank. He yelled at Jerry to finish the preflight and get in. The final preflight task was to check the oil level and Jerry saw an opportunity to make the change in the transponder. When no one was looking, he switched the frequency to 7500 and turned the transponder on. He got in and Joe was right behind him. Jerry wasted no time getting buckled in. He started the engine and asked Joe,

"Could you watch the right side wheel and tire?" He wanted to keep Joe's eyes outside the plane so he could get in the air and get the message out. These radios work on line of sight so the higher they are the farther the message will travel.

When they reached the end of the runway, the engine was warmed up and ready for take off. Jerry asked the guy with the gun, "Hey do you have any aspirin in your bag?" Jerry could also ask him to check the ailerons and flaps on his side.

They climbed out normally – with a full tank of fuel and their mysterious baggage. Any other day Jerry would smile during take off because every take off is a blast, but this time he was distracted, worried about everything outside the cabin, Jerry needed to focus on managing the plane and tasks and most of all, survival.

"You idiot," he yelled. "Do you think I am stupid?" Joe said very agitated. He pointed with his pistol at the transponder and said "You think you're pretty cute, huh, 7500." He turned it off and started kicking it, breaking the knobs and damaging the LCD display – it won't be sending any signals any more. The whole plane shifted with each kick from his heavy boots.

"I thought we had an understanding, he said slowly. "So now you're gonna be a wise guy and I am gonna have to react and do what I don't really want to do." He cocks his arm with the gun back, preparing to strike when he pauses.

Jerry was very busy and distracted by the kicking and yelling but he had his hands full just leaving the ground and climbing out while monitoring the engine and keeping the plane on track. The plane was reacting to the increasing wind by rocking and bucking and Jerry needed to adjust to keep the wings level and stay on course. Joe makes a point of showing Jerry as he turns off the safety on the pistol. The plan to use 7500 on the transponder did not work but Jerry had another good idea.

*   *   *   *

Every plane has an Emergency Locator Transmitter (ELT) that transmits automatically when there is a crash. It sends out a repeating tone on 121.5. They are battery operated, on Jerry's plane right under the pilot's seat.

Jerry dropped his water bottle and while reaching down to pick it up he said,

"Could you check the flaps on your side to make sure they are up all the way?" He turned the ELT on with a flick of the finger. There are 6 D size batteries sending out a constant signal – it should last about 24 hours. He hoped that was long enough to attract some attention.

Up to this point Jerry had been prevented from using the communication radio for any purpose. Normally pilots can monitor the frequencies at the airports they travel near and air to air frequencies so they can talk with other pilots. Pilots also check automated weather reports from airports along the way. The plane was cruising at 95 mph, almost straight north – Jerry thought the destination must be Canada.

"I should have asked you your name." Jerry said after a long pause. He really did not expect a response. "Joe, Joe Smith" he said earnestly.

"Call me Joe" he then requested. Joe was very proud of his name but he worried he may have been too open to the pilot.

Chapter 9

Mandan, North Dakota

A Cadet with the Civil Air Patrol, 70 miles away, was monitoring the radio set at 121.5. He didn't want to do this job; all his buddies were playing with the flight simulator on the other side of the hangar meeting room. He was looking at a 4 year old airplane classified ads magazine dreaming of fast and powerful jets and taking a girl on a date when he heard the familiar beep ... beep ... beep. Somewhere nearby an ELT has been activated. All the guys groaned because just a small percentage of the activations were really emergencies and they knew they had a lot of boring checking to do.

The Civil Air Patrol was an important piece of the Federal aviation infrastructure – they search for aircraft that are missing. The have planes and pilots who communicate with Flight Services to follow flight plans submitted by missing pilots. They have small planes with receivers that can locate the source of the signal. This activation of the ELT triggers a series of activities. The fact that the signal was moving would mean the activation wasn't a crash so quick action with appropriate force would be unlikely—a long shot but there was still a chance they can attract attention. The guy with the gun, Joe Smith, has worked very hard to avoid attention – to blend in and not attract attention. Jerry will do everything in his control to try and thwart Joe and his conspirators.

Chapter 10

Pierre, South Dakota

Lynn and the girls were searching the room that was their prison for resources to either escape or communicate with the outside. The invaders had scoured the room to remove weapons and communication devices. The girls were searching the closet and Lynn was checking the dirty laundry basket. She found a small laser pointer on keychain that was missed by the men. She asked the girls, "How do you signal SOS in Morse code?"

"Is it dot dot dot, dash dash dash, dot dot dot or dash dash dash, dot dot dot, dash dash dash?" "Who cares" said her oldest daughter, "start sending to Mrs. Johnson across the street – she is so nosey, I am sure she is watching our house right now." Lynn went in the bathroom and started signaling with the laser pointer to the house across the street.

Mrs. Johnson's house was at least 300 yards away. Every house in this neighborhood had three to five acres so the houses were not right next to each other. Having some space is a luxury – being able to relax on a patio and have peace and quiet instead of a neighbor watching you through their window.

Lynn put on a positive face with a smile and a squeeze of the girl's hands, but she knows the odds are slim. Lynn must shine it through their windows, into Mrs. Johnson's windows, and not be blocked by curtains; then shine on a wall where Mrs. Johnson must notice it, recognize the signal as a sign for help and figure out the source.

She started signaling, she couldn't see Mrs. Johnson so she focused the laser on one window at a time, a couple of series in each window then on to the next window.   She refused to think about what would happen if Mrs. Johnson came over to investigate — what would these home invaders do to this trusting neighbor.

She smiled again to the girls but worried how long the battery would last.

"Girls, look through your stuff here to see if you can find another thing with a battery for this laser pointer – look for watches, calculators and LED lights."   The girls started digging through drawers and searching under the bed.

They need another plan, Lynn thought as she continued to signal to the neighbor. She was watching for any other neighbor but no movement anywhere – not even a car driving by.

Chapter 11

North Dakota

A bout 35 miles from Canada near a Military operations area the guy with the gun said, "Descend to 500 feet." More action to avoid detection, so this guy must not be with the US government or military. Recently the border patrol started using an unmanned aerial vehicle (UAV), the Predator, to monitor the border. They can fly all day with a team of grounded pilots and another person monitoring the sensors on board. They also use a Rotax engine for power and fly at about the same speed as Jerry and Joe.

Joe Smith? Is that an alias? Probably. It makes no sense to give his real name. Jerry decided to play along.

There is an airport that is actually half in Canada and half in North Dakota. The Canadian and US Customs have a little office there. Jerry wondered if they are going to Canada to pick up something and then bring it into the US. Joe's plan needed a plane and pilot to travel in a manner only this plane can achieve. They needed to be able to land and take off from a space only this plane can handle. Joe had done his research, he had checked the airport — to find the person who was the best at flying fast and low—really low—someone who was great at short rough fields and would handle very light planes. The best pilot for that was Brad Hovelan, but most people thought he had an undiagnosed mental illness and was unstable—Joe needed a pilot who could work under stress.

Jerry also heard there were secret sensors all along the border, guard stations along major roads, military aircraft sorties along the border adjacent to the military operations areas and motion and noise sensors all along the border. The Rotax 912S is a very quiet engine – built to the European noise standards, much quieter than US standards. The engine also has a gear reduction system so the prop spins much slower and thus much quieter.

The plane has an aluminum and steel tube frame, fabric covered and built very light. The whole plane weighed 620 pounds empty—some large snowmobiles weigh that much. Large highway cruiser motorcycles, like the Honda Goldwing, weigh over 900 pounds. This plane does not show up on most radar and it is very quiet—especially at low rpm.

As they got closer to the border Joe gave more frequent instructions, "Left 2 degrees." And then, "Right 3 degrees" They were cruising at 500 feet and then 400 feet, a few miles later 300 feet. Joe kept ordering lower and lower altitude until they were at about 50 feet above the ground. He then demanded, "Slow down, I want slow and as quiet as possible"

"With two people we can safely go 60 miles per hour—that will be about 3500 rpm and still have full control and authority." Jerry explained. Joe kept saying, "Lower." "Slower." then, "Right 2 degrees," while intently watching the terrain.

They were so low they needed to climb to get over small trees and then dive down after passing the trees. Flying this low was very dangerous because of power and telephone lines, cell phone towers and even fence wires that could catch the wheels of a plane and flip it and cause a low survivability crash. Even at 60 miles per hour, the speed seemed very fast because they were so close to the ground. The plane made less noise than a farm tractor and travels as fast as a vehicle on the ground. It should be able to avoid detection.

"Why are we doing this?" "Who are you?" Jerry pleaded while making constant adjustments. Flying was a lot of work. Even though they were going slow there was a high risk something could go wrong and Jerry did not look happy. Joe hoped this would avoid attracting attention as they flew over the border. Jerry wondered whether they would climb even after they got across the border.

Jerry's plane has an ID number that starts with an N; all Canadian planes have identifying numbers starting with a C. The plane would be easily recognized because of the tail number.

Another problem with flying very low is visibility – the pilot cannot see very far ahead—they will be right on top of the landing area before they see it.

"Shut up and fly the plane," Joe shouted as he watched his GPS and the terrain.

"I am a Revolutionist, like in the Colonial War for Independence," he spit out.

Wow, he let his guard down, Jerry was very surprised but he did not have time to gloat. Maybe Joe did that because he was stressed and distracted saying something other than directions and 'shut up'. Jerry finally replied, "Well that's a lot better than a drug dealer or terrorist." He wanted to show empathy, he wanted to let Joe know he understood how important the mission was to him.

Jerry wanted to live but he knew he might have to be a hero.

Joe hoped this mission would make him a hero – stories would be told for generations of this bold and innovative plan to change the political and social landscape of the nation and the world.

Chapter 12

Pierre, South Dakota

T he civil air patrol was getting reports of an Emergency Locator Transmitter across the center of the state from the southern border to the northern border. Because the signal was moving they were less interested in finding the source. Not a crash, probably just someone who bumped it accidentally. They have to follow up though and they will keep track of reports and efforts. A visit from the Civil Air Patrol is embarrassing when they show up at your hangar to politely ask you to turn your transmitter off. Knowing that someone will look for you if involved in a crash is a good feeling, so no one wants to waste the Civil Air Patrol's valuable time. The State Commander has acknowledged four more Emergency Locator Transmitter signals starting since the one that was really an emergency. Reports come from airline pilots who monitor 121.5 and others who just happen to be listening in.

*　　*　　*　　*　　*

Mrs. Johnson, the neighbor across the street, did not notice the laser light on her walls from Lynn and the girls but the home invaders did. Lynn was startled when someone with a drill was removing screws from the barrier out side their door. They were coming. The girls ran into the bathroom and screamed and held on to their Mom when the men burst in. One stood at the door, one grabbed each of her arms and a third began searching Lynn. They found the laser pointer, slapped her and shoved her to the floor as the girls screamed louder and cried. The girls pounded on the invaders who flicked them off like flies and they fell back to their mother.

Lynn felt hate and rage flow through her veins. Her face was red and her eyes were wide open. She was ready to strike back like a mother bear defending her cubs. She realized, however that the time was not right for retaliation – they would get theirs when the time was right. She wouldn't get mad now, she would get even later.

After they left the room without even a word, she wondered how they knew she had the laser pointer. She knew they had made some looking for batteries but she surmised that the noise would be considered normal. As she looked around the room she finally saw the camera near the ceiling by the door. She was embarrassed; with that camera and microphone they had seen and heard everything. "We need another plan, and soon," she said to the girls quietly.

Chapter 13

Canada

"Therefore it is" He shouted. "Do a 180 and get on the ground now!" was his urgent command. Jerry was still at 10-20 feet above the ground, climbing over a slight hill when the guy with the gun shouted his instruction. He gave almost full power, did a climbing left hand steep turn while checking out the runway. It was another skinny grass strip not much wider than a truck's wheel tracks. There was a gravel road along one side and a series of power lines on the other side of the road – not really a factor. Jerry banked left again, lined up with the runway, brought the engine to idle, compensated for the crosswind and put in full flaps almost simultaneously and was on the ground in seconds. He squeezed the hydraulic brake handle and slid to stop about 50 feet from a ditch. Jerry let out a relieved sigh and turned the plane around and taxied back to the center of the runway.

This time two white Chevy Suburbans with heavily tinted windows were there waiting. The men were big and wearing the same dark utility uniforms, helmets, masks, guns and radios. No one spoke as the men spread out and took positions around the perimeter. Two men carried a large aluminum locked case with handles to the plane. There was no room for that in the plane— the only way it would fit was if there was no passenger and Jerry was guessing the guy with the gun would accompany it.

"What is going on here?" "Who are you and what is that?" he yelled pointing at the box. The guy with the gun ran up and took a position between him and the closest group of tough guys.

"Yea, you guys are tough with the big guns – I want some answers," Jerry taunted—he wanted to see how far he could push. Joe turned to face the tough guys and then swung around and hit Jerry hard in the face with his fist. He stumbled backwards and recoiled to swing but stopped when he noticed the gun pointed at his face. Joe was very good—close enough not to miss but far enough away again so Jerry had little defensive options.

"Shut up!" Joe said slowly, "listen to me, you are in a revolution – history will remember your contribution." The men moved closer and listened to every word. Joe looked around -- he knew they were listening so he raised his voice – sounding like a leader.

"What was the United States originally formed on? Freedom and opportunity! Sometimes creation is painful, freedom requires a commitment and sacrifice, who has already sacrificed?"

"We have!!" they shouted in unison.
"Who wants to change the world for the right ideals?"
"WE DO!" They shouted in even louder and held up their weapons.

He then slowed and said softly, "Who has been persecuted for more than 150 years because of who we are and what we believe?"

"WE HAVE" they answered matching Joe's pace.

"Who has a plan for the future of this country?"

"WE have!" They responded well choreographed.

40

A Flying Adventure

Jerry was beginning to see how big this conspiracy was. People fighting for religion or ideology are always more dangerous than those who are fighting as mercenaries. Jerry was still dazed and on his knees and was really scared now; every one of them was willing to sacrifice and likely him along with them. Was this a plan to destabilize the government, hold the country ransom? Would they cause chaos and destroy the economy?

"Who made a commitment with their lives and the lives of their loved ones?" Joe asked as he scanned every eye.

"We have" they replied slowly. They looked each other in the eye as if saying good bye.

"The time is now, don't loose your focus, stick to the plan and take care of yourself. Let's go!" He yelled raising his arms. They all yelled the loudest response, "YEAH!"

Chapter 14

Canada

Inside the aluminum case was a capped stainless steel cylinder with the biohazard symbol all over it. Joe had a key, opened the case and put the cylinder in his duffle bag after removing some empty water bottles to make room. . It had large clamps that held the cap on and looked like a solid secure container but Jerry was still frightened.

Joe was feeling confident—everything was going according to plan. He felt and looked more confident around his friends and colleagues.

Jerry formed a new plan, a much more desperate plan. While Joe was exchanging the steel cylinder Jerry loosened Joe's seat belt straps. He noticed the winds were picking up. A beautiful clear late spring day with high thin clouds – it should have been a perfect day for hundreds of pleasant activities. Jerry resolved that he would do something to either stop Joe and live or stop Joe and die in the process.

They strapped in and taxied to take off. Joe looked somberly out the window. Before take off Jerry did a magneto check—most airplane engines have dual independent ignition and before every flight, pilots check the engine operation by testing each ignition system. The engine will run on one set, but both help the engine produce more power. Airplane engines also have an independent ignition system so if the battery or electrical system fails; the engine would continue to run.

A Flying Adventure

As they rolled and were airborne, Jerry looked back and saw two men in suits and two women get out of one of the trucks. He thought about turning around for another look but felt the gun in his side so he just pulled his lucky hat down lower over his eyes and gave Joe his best 'Screw you' stare. Jerry put in half flaps and slowed the engine down to 3500 rpm and went back to work of flying at 5-10 feet off the ground almost due south.

They were up and down hills and valleys, around trees and over telephone and power lines. If they had engine problems now there would be limited options, the ballistic parachute would not have enough altitude to fully inflate.

There is no dotted line on the ground to indicate the border between the US and Canada. There is no fence like the fence proposed for the US and Mexico border. The only way to tell if you are in Canada or the US is to use a GPS.

The guy with the gun had his fancy GPS, Jerry was following the track on his cheap GPS from the trip north, backwards toward his home. The wind was picking up and there was mechanical turbulence from the hills and trees. Wind is invisible but it acts like a fluid, flowing and tumbling up and over obstructions. A plane will feel like a boat on a choppy lake when the wind is strong. The smaller the boat the bigger the impact – the smaller the plane the more it bounces around. Flying very low as they were, was even more risky in strong wind because the plane can climb or drop 50 – 100 feet in an instant.

Another weather phenomenon that affects aircraft is thermals. The effect is most noticeable on cooler days as the sun warms the dark earth and the air starts to rise. A plane can rise 300-400 feet per minute in these thermal elevators. Gliders use the lift to fly for hours. Heavy planes are barely affected by the thermals but little planes can be pushed around by the rising and falling columns of air. The warm air will rise to a certain altitude where the air is much cooler and then it will mushroom and fall back to the ground. As the plane flies through the thermal the plane will drop several hundred feet per minute then get jerked upwards at 300- 400 feet per minute and on the other side back down at several hundred feet per minute. Jerry planned to hit a thermal hard and cause the guy with the gun to hit his head on the tube hard enough to become disoriented. The bumps were getting stronger and more frequent. Joe was looking forward to being able to climb to smoother air.

Chapter 15

Canada Air Strip

"Can he be trusted?" asked the older man to the other man and two women on the ground as the little plane disappeared on the horizon.

"I trust Joe, he has been in on this project from the beginning," said the younger man. "He has a lot invested too," he added.

"Let's go guys, we have a schedule to keep," said the older woman. The older man said, "What about the pilot – he looked terrible." The older woman explained,"Joe has instructions to dispose of the pilot when complete -- he knows what to do."

They all got back into the SUV. Each seat had a shelf with a laptop computer. The younger man was monitoring Joe's satellite radio, GPS, personal beacon and the transponder in the stainless steel cylinder on a moving map. The older man was in constant communication with a team that was monitoring police and military radio transmissions. The younger woman spoke into her portable radio and said, "Move out guys, go to your assigned locations and keep a low profile." She was also the driver and slammed the truck into gear speeding away from the temporary remote runway.

Everyone else got in their vehicles and literally went their separate ways—at the road intersections two went east and two went west—later each pair would split again. They would maintain contact with portable radios and cell phones.

"Are the planes ready in Pierre?" The older man asked as he prepared a report.

"She was taking care of that." The older woman seemed annoyed he did not know that.

"What about the teams at the destination?" the older man followed up. The younger woman's response was crisp; "You don't need to know about the rest of the plan—do your part and be ready to do what you're told." The Mobile Command Vehicle continued south monitoring the progress of the plane and cargo. Headquarters was also monitoring every vehicle.

Chapter 16

US / Canada Border

Jerry needed more information on their plan. "That speech back there was impressive. We have a lot in common." He said, fishing for more information from Joe.

"You have done a nice job with this flight," he conceded while shifting his grip on the gun.

"Yea, I would like to make our country number one and the rest of the world number two," Jerry said. He was watching Joe out of the corner of his eye to see if he would take the bait.

"I am positive I have never persecuted anyone," Jerry said, testing Joe's reactions further.

"I am all for the ideals you are talking about," he added working to keep the plane level and on course.

"We need true freedom of religion." Jerry said, waiting for a response. Joe was quiet again and Jerry noticed he was sweating and looking a little airsick. Jerry noticed he was wearing long under wear and then he put it together – Joe Smith, persecution for 150 years, religion and long underwear…

"Mormons!" Jerry accidentally said out loud. Joe looked at him with a wide shocked look. "Did I say that out loud?" Jerry said nervously.

"You don't have a clue about what we have experienced, what we have sacrificed, what we are planning. What we are capable of," he lectured while pushing the gun further into his side.

"You're right—there is no way I can know what your life is like. All I can do is try to understand and respect your views" Jerry said sounding sympathetic. No response.

The wind had picked up and they were bouncing around more than ever before.

"It's likely to be smoother up higher, can I climb yet?" Jerry asked as he was bouncing and twisting.

"Not yet" Joe said as his eyes were focused on the portable GPS.

"Maybe there is a way we can work together – I want to be a part of something bigger than me, I want to be appreciated, I want to contribute," Jerry said with all the energy he could muster. He was very busy just keeping the plane right side up and traveling in the correct general direction.

"You're doing fine, go ahead and climb." Joe looked a little 'green'. Jerry increased the engine speed to full throttle and climbed. The thermals were really affecting the plane-lifting one wing and then dropping the other. The wind was twisting the plane and they were rocking and jumping as they climbed to about 2,000 feet above the ground.

"What's the plan?" Jerry asked between attitude corrections. Joe looked at him, considering whether to tell Jerry or not. He relaxed and explained,

"I am not a bad guy, the plan has some negative aspects but the net affect will be positive, 1 step back and 2 steps forward."

"You seem like a person who is a victim of circumstances." Jerry said trying to ingratiate himself.

"There will be some collateral damage but some sacrifice is needed. Sometimes you have to cut out the bad to save the whole," he said thoughtfully.

"What's in the cylinder?" Jerry asked trying to sound supportive.

"We bought some genetically engineered bacteria which will be introduced in the food chain." Joe stated with his eyes becoming slits.

"That's an awesome plan," Jerry said feigning approval. "Everybody takes food safety way too lightly, how can I help?" he added. While they talked, they were getting pushed around by the wind, the thermals and general turbulence. Jerry flew in bumpy weather all the time and he was used to it, but Joe had an uncomfortable look on his face. He was getting a tender stomach.

"Bottled milk," Jerry said, "If a contaminant got in bottled milk it would be delivered very quickly – it is very difficult to track the milk because it always gets mixed and remixed" Jerry had an epiphany – this plan was more dangerous than he even guessed. Milk has a very short shelf life and would be delivered, consumed and sickened and kill people within hours.

Joe looked at Jerry shocked that the plan had been figured out so quickly.

"That's enough!" he said right after a particularly large bump.

Jerry knew he had to put his plan in motion. He had to stop the conspiracy now, at any cost!

"I would like to climb higher to get above this turbulence" Jerry pleaded.

"Yea, go ahead," Joe agreed reluctantly.

Jerry increased power to full and climbed at a steeper angle, the wind was actually stronger at higher altitude and the bumps were harder. At the next big wing lift, Jerry would make his move. Sometimes thermals will lift one wing and not the other putting the plane at a 45 degree angle, or more.

As Jerry climbed, they were hit with the biggest thermal and turbulence that rocked the plane from side to side. Jerry's seat belt was pulled very tight but Joe's seat belt was loose, he hit his head on the structural tube above his head and he yelled "Ouch."

Jerry cracked the ailerons full opposite and the plane rocked to 45 degrees in the other direction—Joe hit his head again and this time he was dazed and released the gun. At that point Jerry switched from a climb to a dive quickly speeding to the VNE or velocity never to exceed. They were climbing at about 60 miles per hour and in a couple of seconds were diving at 120 miles per hour.

There were several seconds of weightlessness, the gun and everything else loose in the plane actually floated in the air. In one smooth action, Jerry grabbed the gun with his left hand, switched off the safety and aimed at Joe's chest and immediately pulled the trigger. He aimed carefully to miss the fuel tank which was right behind the seats.

The bullet entered Joe's left chest, traveled out his right back and missed the planes structure. The recoil on the gun raised it and as Jerry pulled the trigger a second time, the bullet hit the left front side of his head and traveled out the right rear side of his head. This bullet also missed the airplanes structure including the ballistic parachute mounted behind the passengers head.

Blood was everywhere; it splashed off the inside of the door. It stunk like death. Brain matter, bits of skull and hair were plastered on the inside of the plane. Jerry straightened out the plane, switched on the safety, set the gun on the floor and took a deep breath. His hands were shaking and his mouth was dry.

He looked over at Joe to confirm he was dead and was distracted by the sight. He stared a little too long as the plane veered off course.

A Flying Adventure

He reached over Joe and with a shaking hand opened the passenger door. The door swung open as Jerry unbuckled Joe's seat belt. He made a steep right hand turn and pushed Joe out. The plane shifted and yawed to the right when Joe's arm was caught in the seat belt. His body hung outside the plane causing the plane to list. Jerry worked to untangle the corpse but he could not. The plane wobbled in the sky because of the wind and turbulence and thermals and there was a dead body hanging out of the door. His hands continued to tremble.

On the plane's key chain was a very sharp, very small knife—Jerry cut the seat belt, the plane straightened out after Joe's body falls to a wheat field in central North Dakota.

The plane was a mess and Jerry was spattered with blood that was slippery, then sticky and finally crusty. Jerry shook with adrenalin – what just happened? He did it! He did something heroic. Now what? Jerry had a plan to stop the guy with the gun but what now?

Jerry reminded himself to fly the plane. He checked the flight controls and engine—everything was functioning normally. He checked every instrument gauge and as he went through the familiar routine, he relaxed. Jerry was relieved but he knew there was much more to deal with and doubted his abilities.

Joe's bag was still in the plane. Jerry turned 90 degrees west and looked for a lake. About 10 miles west he flew over a medium sized lake. Jerry dropped the satellite phone into the lake and made a steep 180 turn. He pushed the throttle to almost wide open – Jerry checked the fuel level and calculated he would use almost all of his fuel to get home but he needed more speed. He flew about 20 miles east and looked for another lake for the GPS unit. The winds were still strong and the thermals were pumping but he had a plan.

Jerry dropped the GPS in the lake and turned to go home. He could not use the radio or his cell phone—He was certain they were being monitored so he turned the cell phone off. He needed to deal with the bacteria in the stainless steel canister and tell everybody about this plot.

Another member of the Experimental Aircraft Association local club is Bob, he built a beautiful RV 7 kit plane and he owns a Cessna Skylane. Bob worked for a biogenetic seed company in Pierre doing genetic engineering on seeds to develop resistance to diseases, pests and chemicals. He knew a lot about handling biohazard materials -- maybe Bob had a secure place to put this stuff.

He lived on the East edge of town on a small homestead. Jerry could drop the cylinder from the air into his yard and call him later. Jerry realized they could be monitoring him from a satellite so he needed to ditch the plane and get home to rescue his family before the conspirators discovered Joe was dead. Jerry cracked open the door and dropped the canister in Bob's back yard. He then peeled off and headed to another buddies place to launch the rescue of his family.

Chapter 17

Pierre, South Dakota

L ynn moved quickly, she opened the bathroom window and knelt before her youngest.

"We need you to run an errand for us, I will lower you out the window and you need to go to the neighbors and call 911." Their youngest daughter was scared but knew she knew this was something important.

"Can you do that for us?" She nodded her head 'yes'. Lynn leaned out the window with her daughter hanging from her hands.

"Tell them there are at least 8 people with guns," and Lynn let her go. She bounced off the arborvitae and rolled onto the lawn. Kids are made of rubber bands, she got up and waved and ran to the neighbors. The neighbor's backdoor was locked so she rang the door bell. No answer, so she ran to the next neighbor and rang their doorbell—the Godell family was home and listened in awe to the story while dialing 911.

"Send all the Sheriffs and deputies and city police now!" demanded Mrs. Godell.

When her youngest did not return Lynn decided to help her older daughter escape. Lynne would not be able to hold her by the hands out the window so the fall was farther. She tumbled off the shrub and rolled out to the lawn also OK, and ran to the neighbors.

As she was watched her older daughter escape she heard the faint sound of multiple sirens. The police were coming – time to go. With all the firepower downstairs and trigger happy police she did not want to be caught in the middle so she lowered herself out the window while one of the armed men with the power screw driver started removing screws from the door.

She dropped to the ground, twisted an ankle and rolled into the shrub and was scratched on her face and arms. She stood up and limped to the neighbors.

Downstairs one guy monitored the surveillance camera while another monitored other communication including the police scanner. He heard the call to the local police and sheriffs.

"We've been discovered." he yelled. "OK let's get moving," said the leader while packing up their equipment.

Four police cars lined up on the street in front of the house and more cars rolled through the neighbor's back yards surrounding the house.

The police did not see anything unusual—it was quiet and there was no motion. Then they heard engines racing and both the SUV's in the garage burst out simultaneously through the doors. About 3 seconds later the whole lower level of the house exploded out in a percussive type of explosion. Parts of the siding and windows flew a hundred feet through the air. Debris flew out hitting the police cars in the street. The top of the house fell into the basement with a dusty crash and another explosion—this explosion is a huge fireball which sent flaming bits of wood and shingles. The police felt the heat from the flames, as they called the fire department.

Out of the flames and the flying house pieces, one black SUV slammed into a gap between two squad cars and the other turned and drove across three yards in an attempt to escape. The police were outside their cars and shooting at the black SUV's with shotguns and handguns. One police office aimed at the engine with his shotgun—the slug went through the radiator slamming into the ignition unit and the truck rolled to a stop. The other truck bounced across the neighbor's yards and looked like it would get away. A deputy with a rifle aimed for the gas tank –there must be armor in the truck but not the gas tank. The bullet tore a gash in the tank—fuel flowed out creating a perfect air / fuel mixture and when the next bullet hit the steel and made a spark, a fireball destroys the truck and killed everyone inside.

The black SUV that had rolled to a stop between the cop cars didn't open its doors or windows – they never even fired back. The armor and black tinted windows prevented the police from seeing what was happening inside the truck. Then, as the cops were yelling for the occupants to exit, the truck exploded in flying steel and glass with blue – white flames that started the other police cars on fire and knocked the officers on their backs.

The wind pushed the smoke between trees and out across the field. The flames cracked and popped, slapping the sides of the trucks. The officers emptied their little fire extinguishers but they had no impact on the flames. The heat was so intense they finally gave up.

The fire trucks and ambulance rolled in to mop up and protect the neighbor's houses. The police were asking each other "Who are those guys?" The firefighters asked what was in those trucks – nothing normal should burn like that in a truck. The fire chief told the Sheriff, "There was an accelerant in the truck—the victims knew the truck would burn – this was a suicide."

"A suicide? "Are you sure? Were they armed? Did they fire back at us?"

"What the hell is going on here?" The Sheriff said to the officers within earshot.

The other SUV with the home invaders exploded in a secondary explosion of blue white flames.

Chapter 18

Paul's Private Strip, North of Pierre, South Dakota

A n EAA friend of Jerry's named Paul has a landing strip at his rural property with some extra hangar space, Jerry headed there. He did not use the radio and he did a straight in approach. He parked the plane in front of the hangar and ran to Paul's house. Paul didn't believe the story until he saw the cockpit with the blood, brain matter and bullet holes with his own eyes.

"I need to stash this plane and borrow a car and your cell phone," Jerry demanded as he pointed at his plane.

"I need to get to Lynn—she and the girls are being held hostage" he added. Then Paul said, "I'll get the guys together." Jerry didn't take a breath, "Get a message out on the club email list and then we'll meet at the clubhouse."

"You must not have heard yet – there was a huge shoot out about a half hour ago," Paul explained while grabbing his shoulder. Jerry jumped up and ran towards his plane.

"Hey Jerry, wait a second, Lynn and the girls are fine, but your house was destroyed – you gotta call the police and get in contact with them." Paul said while chasing after him.

While he was running Jerry called Lynn's cell phone – but no answer. As quickly as possible he put the plane in Paul's hangar and ran to Paul's car.

Paul drove Jerry to the police station while Jerry explained how to get the conspiracy out in the open.

"These guys are serious and have a ton of influence so we need to tell everyone. They will deny it and they will discredit everyone so we need to use every method possible," he insisted worry lining his face.

"That's why we need the guys in our EAA club to get on the Internet and get the word out."

Paul and Jerry were silent as they imagined what could happen if the bacteria got into the milk supply. How many would die? Babies and old people would likely be affected the most.

Jerry ran into the police station, saw Lynn and the kids in a hall, yelled and ran to hug them. They were all surprised to see him. The police were eager to talk with Jerry and he was eager to tell them the story. He could tell them everything after he has a chance to connect with Lynn and the girls.

"Man, it's nice to see you guys are OK," Jerry said trying to hug them all at once.

"Dad, they blew up our house," said the oldest.

"They hit Mommy," said the youngest.

"You guys are safe now, nothing will happen to you or us." Jerry squeezed the girls and when he closed his eyes he saw Joe's dead eyes staring at him.

"How are you?" Jerry asked Lynn while reaching to brush her hair from her face.

"Just great now that I know you are OK," responded Lynn as her eyes welled with tears.

Police Chief Galen Anderson was an acquaintance of Jerry and Lynn. Galen wanted a briefing; he simply did not believe the story.

"You need evidence, Jerry, where is the plane, the body, the bad guys and the bacteria?"

Jerry leaned forward and pointed as he said, "I will tell you every part of the story – as many people as possible must be in on the briefing. The media, all your officers, record it and publish it on the Internet."

Police Chief Anderson didn't want to allow others in the briefing, "While you are here, we run the investigation."

Jerry refused to talk unless as many people as possible were listening. He wanted all the local media there—everyone.

"Do you have any video we can stream to all the media? Hook it up and let's get rolling." Jerry shouted. The only way this conspiracy would be short circuited was with the light of transparency.

Jerry told the story from the beginning filling in as many exact details as possible—"My GPS will have all the coordinates." He said with confidence. The GPS is in the plane along with a ton of other evidence from Joe Smith's bag. He warned them to expect everyone involved to be discredited. The room was silent as he told the story. Jerry knew he had a believable story because very few questions were asked. Finally, after about 30 minutes of story and questions, Jerry reminded them.

"We need to follow up with Bob and get this shit secured! And get to my plane for the evidence."

Galen sent one squad car with Paul to secure the plane. The Homeland Security officers took Jerry and Lynne to help search at Bob's and one police car went to Bob's workplace just in case he already picked up the hazardous materials and brought it to his employer. One car stayed with the South Dakota Bureau of Criminal Apprehension lab team at Jerry and Lynn's house as they sifted through the two trucks and the burned house. Lynn called her Mom to pickup the kids and take care of them for a while.

A Flying Adventure

When Jerry heard Lynn's story as they were driving to their house, Jerry was amazed at her courage and the way the kids worked together. Jerry was disappointed that their house was destroyed and they agreed they could replace things -- but a family could never be replaced.

They discussed how to proceed, "We are lucky Bob knows about this kind of stuff – I need to call him, can I use your phone?" Jerry left a message with Bob asking him to look in his yard near the hedge for a stainless steel canister. He told him they were on their way and he should call back as soon as possible.

Lynn pulled Jerry's hand and said, "I recommend telling as many people as possible, police, media and the TLA's."

"TLA's ?" Jerry asked with a grin.

"Yea, Three Letter Acronyms, you know, CIA, FBI, ATF, FDA, and CDC." she said with a mischievous smile.

Chapter 19

Border Crossing, Emerson Manitoba

The SUV with the two men and two women that had been at the transfer spot, rolled up to the Emerson Manitoba Border station. They flashed badges and were waved through.

"Who was that?" one guard said to the other. "TSA," said the guard with a shrug. On the road again the team in the SUV from the Transportation Security Administration was shocked when the young man monitoring the planes progress said, "There's a problem."

"Joe's personal location transceiver indicates he has stopped near the North and South Dakota border. The plane is continuing, now turning." The older woman said.

"Scramble our team near there and get more information." she demanded with a look that could've melted steel.

"The satellite phone stopped sending and the plane has changed course again." The younger man reported. The old man slowly said, "Who is going to call Her?"

"She doesn't like disappointments, are we gonna be the loose ends? You know she hates loose ends," the young woman said with a slight tremor in her voice. The truck was very quiet as they considered how the head of this project would react to the news that her son was missing and the project might be derailed.

"The GPS unit has stopped sending, the plane is off our grid, eastbound at the last signal," the young man who was monitoring the tracking devices reported.

"What about the tracking device in the cylinder?" asked the older man.

"Non functional from the very beginning," replied the younger man without even lifting his head from the monitor.

"No one on the Leadership Council will like this," said the younger woman as she tightened her grip on the steering wheel. "What about satellite views? Can we track the plane?"

The older woman lectured, "Look, what happened, happened; now we'll see how good our planning was."

"Let's gather more information, get reports from our teams and proceed. Don't panic, stick to the plan," she said, pounding on the seat in front of her.

The driver watched the road and adjusted the GPS unit to guide her to Pierre, South Dakota. The other conspirators were focused on the portable computers built into the mobile command center. Their faces were serious, they dreaded failure.

Chapter 20

Pierre, South Dakota

Bob looked at his phone and went pale when he saw the name 'Lynn Sherman' on the caller id. Today was the big day – he was nervous but committed to making the change. He didn't know the whole plan. Only that the nation's food supply is vulnerable. He has been told this plan would harmlessly expose weaknesses in food supply security. He didn't pick up but waited for the ringing to end and then checked the message. He sat down clumsily when he heard Jerry's voice and almost dropped the phone when he heard the message. He ran out to the yard and after a couple minutes of searching, found the canister.

This was not the original plan, but it would work. He immediately ran to his truck and drove as fast as possible, without breaking any laws, to the meeting place at the Pierre Airport. He called on his cell phone, "I have the package, I am on my way to the transfer location."

At the airport Bob got right in past the gate with his Angel Flight pass. He traveled to the largest hangar on the corner of the airport farthest from the terminal. After he stopped, he took the single container and put the hazardous materials in 4 Angel Flight Medical Cases. Four pilots had established a cover as Angel Flight pilots carrying transplant organs and people to treatments around the country as a cover for months.

The pilots had their planes ready and were waiting for him. One was a small Piper jet, another was a nearly new

Mooney, another was a nearly new Cirrus SR22 Turbo and a Cessna jet. He did not know any of them, no secret passwords were needed; none of the pilots made eye contact with him.

Without a word the men went about their business. Each pilot took one container and ran to their plane, they all knew their destination. The Cirrus and Mooney were headed to smaller airports in smaller cities, the jets were going further to larger cities. No one talked, no one person knew the other's plan. The common thread was the woman who led the Leadership Council. She was the contact for all these pilots.

Each pilot came from a different part of the country, one from California, one from Wisconsin, one from Ohio and one from Minnesota. Each one would travel to their destination airport and give the canister to another person who would each do their part of the process.

Bob did not wait for all of the planes to depart – he sped home so he could prepare for the next phase of the project. The city was quiet – very little traffic on this Saturday on the streets of Pierre. He smiled a satisfied grin until he turned the corner from the road to his driveway. There was a black SUV parked by his house.

"Probably some kind of salesman," he muttered to himself. After he slammed his car door shut, the two men walked around the corner of the house with guns raised. Bob stopped in his tracks when he saw them. He looked around for an escape route, held up his hands and tensely said, "Just a second guys," while slowly backing to his car.

The two men lead him to their truck, drove him to a remote location. At gunpoint they forced him to dig a shallow grave at the bottom of a dry drainage ditch. As he pleaded and cried for mercy, they each put one round in his head. They then took turns filling in the hole after rolling Bob's body in.

*   *   *   *

At Paul's hangar, where Jerry's plane was stored, the Civil Air Patrol van stopped by the service door. An older man was driving, the young cadet held the radio receiver and said, "Yep, right here."

"Jeez, another false alarm," the Civil Air Patrol Officer said as they knocked on the hangar door. After no answer he walked to the house. Paul's wife Sheryl said, "Go ahead and check the plane, Paul is not here, I'll tell him you stopped by."

Both of the Civil Air Patrol representatives entered the hangar and froze looking at the bloody little plane. A black SUV pulled up quietly. They recognized the Civil Air Patrol van and then the two men stepped out silently. They pulled out their guns and signaled to each other to enter the hangar.

The Officer and Cadet looked at each other in amazement.

"What the hell happened here?" said the Officer. One man dressed in black attacked the Officer with a knife and the other grabbed the cadet and broke his neck—they were both dead instantly. The men from the TSA each took a gas can and started spreading aviation fuel throughout the hangar. They backed out of the hangar and threw a match on the floor and left the door open. A fireball followed them out the door with a violent whoof. They quickly got in the SUV and left the yard, seconds later an explosion blew out the side walls as the fuel tanks in the two planes inside the hangar exploded.

By the time the fire department arrived, the hangar was a smoking pile of bent steel beams. The distorted remains of an all terrain vehicle, small tractor and mower and a seldom used snowmobile were all barely recognizable. The aluminum of the planes had melted and burned—there was no DNA left and no evidence of the conspiracy. The front half of the Civil Air Patrol van was burned, the Cadet and Officer's remains would be identified within a couple of days and their friends and families would be mourning for years.

Chapter 21

Pierre, South Dakota

Police and fire department crews asked, "What is happening? Fires and explosions and 10 deaths in three hours." In Pierre, South Dakota, that was 10 years worth of murders. Bodies were piling up in the hospital morgue, the police Chief called Sioux Falls and Rapid City police departments to request help.

Galen Anderson had been the Police Chief for Pierre South Dakota since he was elected six years ago as a young - gung ho law and order candidate. He had mellowed and accepted the reality that life was fuzzy, the line between good and bad was indistinct and enforcement of laws can be variable.

He had attended high school with Jerry, Jerry was two years older and Lynn was a year younger. Knowledge can be a burden—everyone in a small town knows each other   they remember the anecdotes, positive or negative forever. Small towns are where a 45 year old guy can be forever the guy who scored the winning touchdown or allowed the winning touchdown. Small towns are where a 70 year old man will be known as the son of Lars. In a small town people remember a woman's maiden name longer than her married name.

Galen was never a part of any clique in high school; he went to college at the local community college and worked as a security guard. He joined the military because there were not lots of other jobs and he wanted to travel. He ended up working security for less money at exotic places living in less than great conditions. Galen learned teamwork, how to get along with others, how to listen to people and let them tell their stories. He came back to Pierre because his family was there and he wanted to give back to his community.

He got a patrol officer job with the city, worked his way up to Sergeant and then was elected Chief; but he was still considered the new kid. He could have been described as the Andy Griffith of his time. He knew all the modern crime fighting technology but found the most effective techniques were the old ones. He had an uncanny ability to tell when someone was lying; he just gets a gut feeling. He could not tell you how he knew but he was almost always right.

He had married late in life, just five years before, but his wife was diagnosed with ovarian cancer and died before their second anniversary. Friends and co-workers tried to introduce him to women, but he wasn't interested. He spent too much time at the casinos and spent too much money gambling on sports as a distraction.

He was tall, six feet, two inches, and carried extra weight around the middle; he used to be in great shape but had not been taking good care of himself recently. He had blond hair and a thin face, lately there were dark bags under his eyes. Between the stress from work and the misfortunes in his personal life, he had been on a bad run the last few years.

He had a team of officers—like most teams his team had a combination of strengths and weaknesses and it was a challenge to keep them functioning well. Like most teams, there was conflict, keeping everyone pulling in the same direction was a constant battle.

They respected him and followed his orders without question. They know they cannot lie to him. The only complaint they had would be his lack of a sense of humor he was a very serious man.

Jerry told a fantastic story—it was the truth but the truth can be harmful. Who ever knows what the whole truth is. Galen reassembled the media and other law enforcement leaders for a briefing.

"Look guys we have a problem, maybe a huge problem." Galen explained. "I need you to keep a lid on this for at least two more hours, give us until 4:30 and then go ahead and release the news to everyone." He pleaded.

"We have this under control, we know what their plan is but we do not want to create a panic so can you guys pledge to keep this under wraps for just two hours, 120 minutes. Just stall a bit—you TV guys can still make the six PM news. I want the news out but let's hold off." They all grumbled but agreed.

Galen assembled his team and sent them off with assignments to confirm the known and gather evidence while protecting themselves and the citizens – that was the short term plan.

"Good thing the two TSA agents are in the area doing an audit of the local airport – they volunteered to help and their help is appreciated."

Chapter 22

Pierre South Dakota Police Headquarters

erry and Lynn had a strong sense of urgency. They had first hand experience with the deadly precision and dedication of the conspirators. They and Galen and all of the officers were worried. Bob was not home, his car was not there and they could not find the canister. The Officer gave them a ride back to the Police Station.

"We must get to Paul's place as soon as possible!" Jerry told Lynn as he put his arm around her.

"You gotta see the plane, it's a mess. I've got Paul and the rest of the EAA guys spreading the word on this conspiracy." Jerry continued to explain as he looked out the window of the police car.

Galen had asked the judge for a search warrant and sent Jerry and Lynn with the TSA guys for a ride to Lynn's Mother's house to reunite them with their children. Afterward, they were asked to go to Paul's place to secure the scene until a forensic unit could get out there.

Lynn had arranged for her Mom to watch the kids for a while longer– she picked them up at the Police station while Jerry was telling the conspiracy story.

Jerry and Lynn got in the back seat of the black SUV with the two TSA agents. They were big guys dressed in black with ear pieces and dark sunglasses. They looked like twins, dark brown hair cut very short and almost identical muscle builds.

"Hey guys, can you swing us by Paul's hangar so I can show the plane to my wife?" Jerry asked. The two guys said in unison, "NO."

"Come on guys –it's a little detour," he pleaded smiling at Lynn. The guy in the passenger seat was working with a portable GPS unit. When Jerry saw it he went pale. It was the exact same unique type of GPS that Joe Smith, the hijacker, had used on his trip to Canada. His breathing became shallow and frequent.

Jerry looked at Lynn with a desperate look on his face, Lynn started to say,

"What's…" Jerry held up a hand to signal 'don't say anything.'

"Hey guys, this is not the way to Lynn's parent's house, and we are not on the way to the hangar," Jerry questioned while reaching into Lynn's purse.

"Yeah, the road is closed ahead—this is the way, trust us," the driver said. The two TSA agents gave a knowing look and nod to each other.

Jerry fumbled for Lynn's phone; he could find the redial function because her phone is the same as his. The last number dialed was the Police Chief, Galen Anderson's personal cell phone. Jerry looked at Lynn's eyes and motioned to the purse. They moved a bit closer together to hide the phone.

Galen answered the phone,"Hello, Hello?' No answer but he heard sound in the background.

"Hey guys you better slow down; this is a 65 mph speed zone here on highway 61," Jerry said with a positive lilt in his voice.

"Shut up," they said in unison.

Jerry tried to sound ignorant, "OK guys not a problem just trying to help out, you know, we can get back to Paul's by turning right on County Road 65 here."

"Shut up asshole!" shouted the guy in the passenger seat. "We ain't going to your Mom's and there is nothing at the hangar for you to see," he sneered.

"Shut up," said the driver to the passenger with a disapproving look.

"I don't care, this piece of shit killed Joe, I wanna do him now—you can kill the bitch," said the guy in the passenger seat as he moved his hand to his gun and shifted in his seat so he could turn and watch them.

Lynn was ashen and shaking as she squeezed Jerry's hand so tight the ends of his fingers where now white.

"So what's the deal, you're gonna take us out to the country and kill us? Bury us?—there is nowhere to hide, you'll never get away with this," Jerry said trying to bluff guys who could never be bluffed.

*   *   *   *   *   *

"You guys come from the west on highway 61—black SUV with Federal License plates," Galen told the Sheriff Deputies. "We'll come from the east" he added.

"Remember do not use the regular broadcast frequencies – they are monitoring—oh, and be very careful—wait for backup," was his final warning as the car squealed around the corner.

Two cars approached from the west and two cars followed from the east at a very high rate of speed. Galen and the other squad car were on them first—they turned off their lights and siren and waited for the black SUV to come upon the road block. As the SUV slowed down, the two following cars turned on their lights and sirens and rolled up less than a car length away. The black SUV pulled over and when the driver put the car in park, the doors unlocked automatically.

Jerry and Lynn dove out and rolled down the ditch while the police and deputies approached with guns drawn.

While Jerry and Lynn crawled through the tall grass, the police and Deputies were about 20 feet away with their weapons drawn and aimed at the truck. A large - extremely white explosion blew the doors and windows of the vehicle out. The explosion knocked the police officers backwards and the flying steel and glass cut one of the officers. The two other officers were injured in the fall. Huge plumes of white smoke poured out the broken doors and windows. After the percussive explosion a fireball blast enveloped the vehicle and its occupants. The white smoke turned grey then black and smelled like a combination of burning plastic and flesh. The noise made Jerry and Lynn jump and duck. They all backed away from the heat but they kept watching to see the charred black human shapes in the front seats.

None of them could hear well afterwards because the noise from the explosion was so loud. The guys in the SUV had not fired a shot. They did not try to escape.

There was a little more evidence this time. The two guys had released their identities, the truck had Federal plates, there was video of the two men and they had identified themselves as Transportation Security Agency agents. Finally, some leads to follow.

Chapter 23

Salt Lake City, Utah

In a nondescript warehouse on the outskirts of town, in an industrial park development, between a drywall contractor and a carpet cleaning company was another company – Smith and Associates. The building had six satellite dishes and a huge generator on the roof. The doors in front and in back were reinforced and very different than the other business.

Inside, three rows of technicians monitored audio and video from vehicles and agents around the country. The people who worked there told their friends that they work for a call center – selling long distance coverage. Women held all the roles, except for security and cleaning, at Smith and Associates. Women got their jobs mostly through nepotism. Employees could trace their heritage and work history together. This was a very low key operation. The women didn't even tell their husbands what they actually did. The work environment created an environment of competition.

"We need to tell her another truck is down" one of the techs said while making back up copies of the video files. "Forget about telling her, she already knows," said her partner as she looked over her reading glasses.

"That's the third one today on Operation Mothers Milk," she added as she swiveled her head to see if anyone could hear them. Another technician was reporting to her supervisor, "There is significant chatter on our hot words, 'Mormons and bacteria'—targeted in South Dakota – we gotta tell her."

The manager on duty yelled out, "OK everyone, I want a summary report within 10 minutes from each of you working on project Mothers Milk."

In a conference room in the middle of the space, a multimedia screen showed four different reports simultaneously. There were three other offices on a video conferencing system— one labeled Maryland, one labeled Leadership Council and one labeled Washington DC. The light was red indicating the message was being received but the rooms were dark to shield the speaker's identities.

The woman at the Leadership Council reported, "I already heard about Joe, I don't want to hear about any other screw ups, I want a plan and I want results!"

The associates in Maryland and Washington indicated affirmative in unison.

"Madam Leader, we've lost seven agents, counting your son. We have a Strategic Mobile Field Command group on the ground near Pierre and we have begun the discrediting and obfuscation process," reported the agent from Maryland in a rapid fire, perfectly enunciated delivery.

"Keep in mind we are still on track with the time line and the project is Green," reported the associate from Washington.

"Right, but only due to dumb luck, I want a project manager that can develop a plan and follow a plan. We reward for results, not this shit," shouted Madam Leader, throwing a pile of paper in front of her into the light and on camera.

"Madam Leader, everything is under control," a female voice from behind her said. "I will personally manage this project – I assure you we will use any means necessary to complete this project – including any capital expenses." She said with a scowl. Capital expenses meant deaths – people who make huge mistakes run the risk.   Big rewards and big costs.

"OK, you can take over but no more loses, no more exposure, we need discipline and commitment" after a pause she looked at the younger woman and quietly said, "I am uncomfortable allowing you to become exposed to this risk…. but, this project is crucial and must be completed on plan."

In the Mormon Church, the men run the religion, businesses and social programs and the women run the politics.

Madam Leader was a trim - tall mature woman.   She was a hard leader who was unforgiving of mistakes and very stingy with praise. She always wore a suit coat and matching skirt in various shades of grey. She also always wore a white high neck cotton blouse with a pearl necklace. She had worked her way up the organization through grit, determination and willingness to set up and blackmail anyone and everyone who got in her way.

From the beginning of the church, over 150 years ago, the men made the headlines but the women had the power. They developed relationships to establish power, brokered influence and manipulated people to get what they wanted.

She had been the first to push the organization to utilize modern electronic communication methods. The whole organization was recorded and every inch was covered by audio and video cameras.   Video brought her most of her good subjects – she enjoyed watching and dissecting video. Her office was set up to simultaneously monitor 8 different video feeds or recordings. She could zoom, run slow motion or change camera views anywhere in their network and.

She was married and had two grown children. Her husband was an overweight man who managed a construction company. Lately she had been wondering how two smart and talented kids could come from such a slow, sloppy and stinky father. She was glad he had another wife – the house keeper.

Madam Leader had no interest in any carnal union with her husband. At one time he was bearable and she had a genuine affection for him but he didn't grow and change like she had. She kept him around just to maintain appearances. She was in control of her emotions in a practiced manner. She could smile and make small talk while calculating her moves. With a word she could have any one of them killed and disposed of without a trace.

She was very proud of her children—they had adapted to the family business like her Grandmother and Great-Aunts. She was proud of her daughters rise up through the Leadership Council. She was eagerly waiting and even encouraging her to give her a granddaughter soon.

She had great aspirations for her son and in her position she could make just about anything she wanted happen for him.

Her only hobby was watching video. At home she spent most of her time in her home office reviewing video. She was always looking for opportunities to manipulate people. That's how she got and maintained her power. She looked for human weakness. Sooner or later there would be an opportunity to exploit a person for her own ends.

Chapter 24

Pierre, South Dakota

Police Chief Galen, Jerry and Lynn and the three other officers were standing around the only remaining police cruiser that wasn't damaged, watching the SUV burn. They stood silently on a quiet highway with the background of the wide prairie and billowing smoke from the burning SUV. The officers all had a weary slouch, their uniforms were dirty and several had ripped pants or dirty hands and faces.

Only one squad had a fire extinguisher—the others had emptied theirs on the SUV's at Jerry and Lynn's house. They stood in a circle; Jerry and Lynn were arm in arm when Galen finally spoke, "What the hell is this?" he asked rhetorically.

"OK, we have Mormons and Homeland Security in a gigantic conspiracy to attack the food supply, and along the way, seven agents got killed." Galen kicked some rocks on the road, took off his hat to wipe his forehead and tugged at his pants.

Everyone was silent because they too are trying to understand the scope. Jerry then said, "These guys didn't even fire back – they had guns but…"

"The other guys at your house didn't fire back either," said one of the Deputies to the Police Chief. "OK, if this is so big, how do we proceed?" asked another police officer as he walked closer to Galen.

"This must be bigger than just food safety—what is worth so many lives?" asked Galen while he searched the horizon.

Galen was a good leader, he considered everyone's input before he made his decisions. Enough retrospection, this was the time for action.

"OK, Jerry and Lynn, you get outta here right now and don't use any internet, radio, cell phones or go anywhere a camera might be." Jerry and Lynn looked at each other and knew they had to fly. They could borrow a plane from a friend and go to small airports and find people that could keep them safe.

"We need help, big help."

"Who hates Homeland Security?"

"Who would like to see Homeland Security be embarrassed?"

"What agency did Homeland Security take budget or power from? That's who we want to help," Galen said, thinking out loud. He was about three steps ahead of the other officers but only about a half step ahead of Jerry.

"The CIA works mostly overseas and NSA is too small, the military could help but they are too slow, The Attorney General and the Justice Department can't help now—you need tactical and national so any State enforcement agency would not work—that leaves the FBI." Jerry said to no one specifically. Lynn grabbed his arm, "Think about the kids, you are not qualified for this, this is out of your league, don't even think of doing any more, you're not a hero," she said directly to Jerry.

"You are already involved enough, Jerry. This is outside you area of expertise, you had a nice run, you can live on this story for ever—leave this for the professionals." Galen said trying to be firm but recognizing Jerry's significant accomplishment. "You've been through enough already."

In the distance they heard the sirens from the fire truck and ambulance.   Galen turned to his officers, "Buck, you drive to Sioux Falls and tell the story to the FBI there, do not take the interstate highway—remember there are those cameras over the roads, do not use your cell phone, do not use your radio either, and do not stop for any reason."   Buck ran to his car and took off for Sioux Falls. His was the only car that did not have body damage and had all its windows.

"Jimmy, give Jerry and Lynn a ride to get their kids." Galen said to Jimmy as he put his hand on Jimmy's shoulder. To Jerry and Lynn he said, "And don't tell anyone—even Jimmy or me where you are going."

The fire truck rolled to a stop; the volunteer firefighters quickly began spraying fire retardant on the fuel assisted flames. The Fire Chief ran up to Galen and said, "This is screwed up— they used an accelerant—remember high school chemistry when we lit stuff on fire—remember the magnesium? How it burned so hot and bright?"   Galen nodded, paying very close attention.

The Fire Chief continued, "I have found evidence that the explosions in the vehicles was remotely detonated and the accelerant caused almost total destruction of the vehicle, the passengers and additional evidence—we don't have much to work with, the damage was so bad."

"Yeah, this is screwed up –they didn't fire back—none of them fired back." Galen said puzzled. "So, if the trucks were blown up remotely, is it a good guess that there was video and audio in and around the truck?"

"Probably," admitted the Fire Chief, "But we will know more in a couple of days after the State Crime Lab gets the trucks in their lab."

"We don't have a couple of days," said Galen.

Chapter 25

A Private Airstrip South of Pierre, South Dakota

J erry and Lynn picked up their kids and told their Grandparents to take a trip but not use their credit cards or cell phones and tell no one where they were going. Jerry drove to another flying buddy's private airstrip, Chip Jeffries' place. Chip has a Piper Archer, a four person aircraft that has speed and carrying capability. He babied that plane – it was in just about perfect shape. It was mostly glossy white with a bright red stripe on the fuselage and thick stripes on the wings. Chip had already heard about Jerry's adventure through the EAA email list.

"Chip, I won't tell you where we are going and I suggest you leave town too." said Jerry as Lynn was putting the kids in the plane. Chip responded nervously, "Hey, take care of my plane, it's full of fuel and airworthy." "Just bring it back in the same condition with full fuel and then you can owe me!" Chip said with a smile.

"Have you guys seen the TV news?" Chip asked while he was checking the propeller blades. Lynn and Jerry looked at each other with a quizzical look. He turned on the little TV in his hangar and they watched about two minutes of CNN. They quickly learned about the corruption in the Pierre Police Department and that Jerry was wanted for being a terrorist and having a dirty bomb.

"Dang, you're the first terrorist I've met." Chip said to Jerry with a smirk. He turned the television off with a "hrumph".

A Flying Adventure

Chip and Jerry met about 10 years ago at the EAA chapter meeting and were good friends from the start.

Jerry earned his private pilot license in a Piper Warrior, and was very familiar with the plane – it had been a couple of years since he flew one but he had the check list and Lynn would help with procedures and operate the navigation radios. The Warrior was very similar to the Archer. After a thorough preflight Jerry started the engine.

This plane had a 180 horsepower engine, a low wing four seat aircraft that could cruise at more than 130 miles per hour miles per hour. It used 9 to 11 gallons of aviation gasoline per hour depending on speed and had a range of about 400 miles. They would need an isolated airport, turf or asphalt, with fuel and without any cameras.

Jerry had paused while checking the plane and was looking into the distance. He sees Joe's eyes and blood spatter when his mind wanders.

"Where are we going, Jerry?" Lynn asked as she was packing the girl's Hello Kitty and Horseland luggage. She noticed he was quiet and slowed down the preflight inspection.

"We will need fuel in about 400 miles, somewhere remote, somewhere no one would ask any questions." Jerry said jerked back to reality. "Any suggestions?" he asked as he was sorting through the sectional maps.

"Jerry, are you OK to fly? You seem distracted, and no wonder, after what you experienced today most people are affected by that type of traumatic event."

"Most of the time I am great. I am just glad to be alive and I am so grateful you and the girls are safe. I'll be OK if I just keep busy and keep my mind occupied." Jerry replied earnestly.

Under normal circumstances a pilot would plan the flight with a route and weather briefing but there was no time.

"The sparsest population is Arizona and New Mexico, I think we can find a place to hang out, let's head south." Lynn suggested.   Chip had some old sectional maps, they were out of date, by a couple of years, but that was all they had and that would have to do.   By this time the engine was warmed up, seat belts and door checked and they had completed the preflight checklist.   Chip had a runway on his 40 acre farm.   It was an undulating, smooth runway with a dog leg about 2/3rds of the way down.   There was a small hill on both ends so they were able to get a good start.

The Piper was not a short - field - take - off plane—it needed about 1200 feet to get off the ground at full gross weight, the dog leg is about 1200 feet down the runway.   They taxied down to the end of the runway and ran one wheel right to the edge of the runway and gave full power with one notch of flaps. Jerry pulled back the yoke to keep the nose wheel light.   The airspeed increased, 20, 30, 40 knots – they need 60 knots to take off and the dog leg was approaching quickly.   The plane performed as advertised, lifted off just before the dog leg and flew in ground effect until the airspeed increased to safe climb out speed, then they made a heading south and west.

They did not turn on the GPS, and they kept the communication radios set to automated weather reporting only. They could fly incognito for hours.   No flight plan was needed because they would be flying under visual flight rules; they would not need to talk with air traffic controllers because they would not be near any high altitude airways or going to any controlled airports.

"How are you guys doing back there?" Jerry asked his kids after about five minutes aloft.   They had flown with their Mom and Dad many times—they thought this was another great adventure—first the bad men at their house and now a fun flying adventure. At least they knew their parents were safe.

After a couple of more minutes in the air, Jerry said, "If the media thinks I am a terrorist and Galen is corrupt, how do we fight that?" That was a rhetorical question—there is only one way to fight media misinformation.

"I bet Homeland Security and the Mormons are spreading these lies," he added. Lynn just sat there with a frown on her face then said, "Jerry, there is nothing you can do to help Galen, you've done enough, think of your family!"

"The best way to fight the mis- information is with evidence. Right now they have none. Since my plane and all the evidence in it was destroyed, they have no solid evidence." Jerry explained.

"You would probably be in the way so…" Lynn started but did not finish.

"Remember the time you bought that expensive bicycle – you were going to be the best bicycle racer. Then you bought all those wood working tools – you said you were going to make furniture for us," she reminded him.

Jerry banked the plane in a left hand 180 degree turn back to Chip's house and runway.

"Oh no, we can't go back, those men are killers and they are everywhere, you are just a guy, you have no training, no special skills. I love you but ..." Lynn pleaded.

"OK, take this plane and the kids and I'll give you half of my cash; there is an airport at Broken Bow, Nebraska, it borders a large Indian Reservation. Go there, store the plane in a rented hangar and get a hotel room—don't pay with a credit card. A couple of days and this will be over, turn off your cell phone." She turned away with a distressed look on her face.

"Turn it back on at Noon tomorrow – keep it on for just five minutes and then turn it off. If I do not call, move to another place and expect a call the next day," Jerry said with a determination Lynn had not seen in a long time.

"I gotta do this, this is important to the country, our community and our friends." Jerry explained further.

They landed back at Chip's, he had already left. Jerry gave Lynn a hug and a kiss then a kiss for each of the girls. He lingered during each hug, smelling their skin and hair, trying to make a memory of their warm skin and shining eyes. They were very quiet; they knew they were all in danger.

Jerry watched Lynn taxi and take off – the take off was perfect, the plane was lighter and got off the ground in plenty of time. He watched her take off and circle to the southwest and then when he could not hear her any more, he walked to the hangar. Chip kept a spare key on a nail underneath the rubber flap of the main door seal. Jerry unlocked the service door and checked Chip's toys. He had an ATV, a Harley Davidson motorcycle and a 250cc dirt bike. The key was already in the small motorcycle so Jerry pulled it out, as he did he noticed— low fuel. He searched for a gas can, found one and filled the motorcycle.

From Chip's hangar phone Jerry called Galen's personal cell phone. "Hello, this is Police Chief Anderson," Jerry said. "Meet me at Frankenstein's," and hung up.

Galen smiled and said, "I'm sorry but you have the wrong number," then hung up. He then walked out of his office and said to the Dispatcher, "Are the guys still out at Bob's searching his place?"

"Yes, they've been there about 30 minutes," the Dispatcher replied while making notes of the location of the operation cruisers.

"OK, I'm going out there—we need evidence," he said loud enough for everyone to hear as he was gathering his utility belt with night stick, weapon, handcuffs, pepper spray and radio. As he was reaching for the door, the Dispatcher said, "Chief! Urgent phone call for you, the Assistant Attorney General on the line."

Galen rushed back to his office and closed the door behind him. The Assistant Attorney General said, "Hello Galen?"

"Yeah," Galen said.

"What the hell is going on there? Don't answer, you don't have time --- I just got word that Homeland Security will be there in 15 minutes to arrest you."

"Shit!" Galen responded as he stood up.

"Thanks," he added and hung up the phone. The Assistant Attorney General was a good friend, the two of them had worked together a few years ago. He took a huge risk warning Galen.

A knock on the door and the Dispatcher poked her head in—"Chief, we've been looking at video from the airport and we spotted Bob's pickup going in about 11:30. We got a list of flights out today and there were four Angel Flights around Noon." Galen felt the hair on his arms rise and he asked,"Any connection to milk plants?"

"We are still looking, but one flight destination was the Mayo Clinic in Rochester, Minnesota, and there is a large milk processing facility about 10 miles away," the Dispatcher said with urgency.

"Great work, get more info on the others. When the FBI get here give them, and only them, the information, if anyone else comes, tell them nothing, tell everyone here, only give information to the FBI, no one else, this is important," He said with his more authoritative voice.

"Absolutely Chief!" said the dispatcher to Galen who rushed out.

Galen went out the back door to get an unmarked car; he would leave his personal truck parked in front. He looked over the parking lot -- four cars with broken windows – two of those had body damage and two had partial paint burns. There goes the budget for next year, he would have to make a specific plea to the City Council for more funds and he hated that part of the job.

He looked around to see if anyone was watching and quickly got in the unmarked four door sedan, a Ford Taurus, and drove out of the parking lot. He was looking for any vehicles that were following him. Galen went to the Hardee's drive through and saw another dark sedan, a Ford Crown Victoria with two guys wearing sunglasses in the front seat, parked a half block away. After he received the food, he drove out, and they followed. He confirmed they were following him, he drove while eating and got in line for a car wash. The car wash had a 180 degree turn that was out of sight from the street. He turned away before going in the car wash and cut back through an alley. He climbed a curb, drove across a strip of grass and squeezed the car between two telephone poles that separated two office buildings. The guys in the car waited for all the cars to come out of the car wash, when the Chief's car did not show, they made a call on their radio, "We lost the target, proceeding with search."

"He's probably going out to the drop zone—I am sending a map and details to your vehicles computer," said the younger TSA guy in the white SUV. The Mobile Strategic Command vehicle—the same white SUV loaded with monitoring and communication equipment held the four people who where at the transfer air strip in Canada. They were monitoring the other Homeland Security and TSA agents and the phones at the police station.   They were also in constant communication with Washington DC and Salt Lake City.

*   *   *   *

In high school people get odd nicknames—Galen had heard that Bob's nickname was Frankenstein because he had a particularly high forehead—this was accentuated by his receding hairline.   Galen smiled because he knew Bob hated the nickname, and then he made a disgusted face because the video evidence indicated that Bob was part of the conspiracy.

He finished his fast food meal while escaping from the Homeland Security agents but had one regret—"I gotta eat better food." he said out loud to no one.

Chapter 26

Pierre, South Dakota

T he phones were ringing constantly but not from people reporting crimes. News crews were calling to arrange interviews and trying to gather information. CNN was running pictures of the Police Chief Galen Anderson and Jerry Sherwood. The sound was down on the TVs at the station, the caption read "Terrorists." Someone turned the volume up and heard reports from Washington that corruption was throughout the entire Pierre Police Department and Jerry was the ring leader. Fox News and MSN were both reporting that Jerry had developed a dirty bomb and was planning to deliver it some where in the next couple of hours.

Television stations in Sioux Falls and Rapid City were reporting Jerry and Lynn's house was destroyed when a bomb Jerry was building exploded accidentally in their basement. Online news sites were also reporting that Jerry and Lynn, the co-conspirators, were on the run and citizens were instructed to call Homeland Security if they saw either of them.

Washington DC

At the FBI headquarters, in the media monitoring room there was a louder buzz than normal and many puzzled faces. The Media Monitoring room is a large open office-type room with agents monitoring media. More precisely they were monitoring computer programs that were monitoring video and audio, tracking keywords and analyzing in real time, the words and images being broadcast. They also tried to correlate these firestorms of specific names and words to identify sources and track the timelines.

"How did we miss this plot?" said the Manager of Media Monitoring to her Director. They were video conferencing.

"We think this is a hoax and the source may be within a government agency," said the Director matter-of-factly. The Manager of Media Monitoring was startled; she had a puzzled look on her face for a second but went quickly back to the confident relaxed face she rehearsed in the mirror. She said, "We can do an analysis and report back in 4 hours."

"You have 30 minutes- this is too big and is changing too fast to wait," the Director demanded, turning to leave.

"Report only to me, no matter who calls."

The Manager of Media Monitoring furrowed her brow, this time for a few seconds and said hesitantly, "But our procedures specifically require we also report to your leader and Homeland Security."

"OK, you are correct, of course" said the Director stepping closer to her. "Please send a copy to our Senior Director but the requirements do not say <u>when</u> we report to Homeland Security—hold that report for four hours. Any questions?" the Director asked, even though he did not want or expect any questions. He quickly turned and walked away as an aide ran up and gave him a phone and a file.

The directions were clear – the "why" was not revealed. Most of what they do in Media Monitoring is requested without knowing what they really were looking for or why they wanted the information. Everything in the FBI was on a 'Need to know' basis and she accepted that they did not need to know.

She scrambled out of her secure office and made a general announcement to the entire room, "All team leaders report to the briefing room now." Once inside she laid out the plan to analyze the timeline and source of any and all media reports related to the conspiracy in South Dakota.

*   *   *   *   *   *   *

There is a well hidden group in the FBI that reports directly to the Deputy Director that monitors Homeland Security. They know there is probably a similar group in Homeland Security that monitors the FBI. The Deputy Director visited the Hotel Sierra workgroup as they are known; they work in a very small office with the oldest furniture. The walls are dirty and scratched, even the name on the door has mismatched letters. Their group is an example of deception inside of deception. They want no one to have any desire to find out about their group, even inside the FBI.

The Deputy Director addressed the group of experienced analysts and agents in their work space because they do not have a private meeting room. He signaled for the door to lock and his associates swept the room for listening devices. After he got the OK from the technicians and they left, the Deputy Director began.

"There is something very suspicious going on in South Dakota right now. We believe TSA and Homeland Security are involved in some sort of operation—certainly some sort of smear campaign, but for what reason? I don't need to remind you that there are no coincidences and there are often several layers of deception in conspiracies." On a white board he drew three interlocking rings and then a fourth separate ring. He continued, "Here we have three separate organizations. Where they intersect is likely this conspiracy; but we believe there is a fourth organization which is influencing all three. You need to find the coincidences, the correlations, any connection between Homeland Security and the activities related to this conspiracy."

"Dig for information from non traditional sources, we believe the media may be part of the conspiracy—maybe unwitting, but still be very skeptical of their reports. I need a report in 30 minutes. This is crucial and should be considered 'All hands on deck' so put all our resources on this project." He looked up and into the eyes of the team and asked, "Any questions?" He expected no questions and indeed he would not answer any questions even if they were asked. The phrase "Any Questions?" means discussion is over, get to work. There were times for open discussion; this was not one of them.

Chapter 27

Pierre, South Dakota

erry rode the dirt bike as fast as he could on the gravel roads from Chip's house. Gravel roads turned into paved roads after a few miles. He was traveling from Southwest of Pierre all the way through town to Bob's place, Northeast of Pierre. Jerry negotiated the traffic until a dark sedan pulled out of a blind alley and forced him to slam on his brakes. He skidded to a stop -- feet from the car with tinted windows and two men wearing sunglasses. They could not recognize him because he had on a full face helmet, but he recognized them. He shook his fist at the guys and took off around the stopped car in the middle of the road. If the conspirators were all over town his plan was getting even more dangerous. Maybe he should have stayed with Lynn and the girls.

A few minutes later, he was at Bob's; he snuck into the hangar, checked the fuel in the plane and opened the door. As he was pulling the plane out, Galen poked his head around the corner of the hangar door.

"Hey Jerry, it's about time you got here, I have new information and a plan," Galen cheerfully announced. "One of the shipments went to a large milk plant near Rochester, Minnesota." Jerry pulled faster and harder on the plane and said "Get in, let's go!"

Bob's plane was a Cessna 182 Skylane, an older four seat high-wing plane that would be able to make the flight from Bob's turf strip to Rochester quickly and comfortably. The plane was in great shape, the paint color was straight from the late 70s

92

-- stripes in mustard yellow, bright gold and earth tone orange. Jerry said, "I am really disappointed in Bob, it's hard to believe he is involved in this mess – I don't feel bad taking his plane."

This plane was faster than the Piper – "We will be in Rochester in two and a half hours," Jerry bragged to Galen as he patted the engine compartment.

He got into the plane and said, "Let's get the hell out of here!"

Jerry started the plane and taxied to the end of the grass runway. He did a preflight run up and noticed Galen's men walking down the runway towards them. The engine was barely warmed up but Galen said, "Enough screwing around, Go, Go now!" Jerry gave full power and they rumbled down the runway and lifted off halfway down. Galen's men on the runway ran to the edges.

Jerry normally flew straight to gain altitude, but this time he banked left and headed east, low to the ground. They both saw the caravan of dark vehicles followed by a plume of gravel dust heading towards Bob's house. They both hoped the men in the government trucks did not see them take off.

The crew knew they had to protect Galen so they put the dirt bike in the hangar and closed the door and hustled back to work gathering evidence. When the Homeland Security task force arrived, the officers denied seeing Galen, and when they were asked about Bob's plane they said Bob must have taken it—he was still missing. Luckily, they did not notice any plane taking off.

Chapter 28

Washington DC FBI Media Monitoring Unit

W e are done," said the Senior Analyst proudly as he handed over about 30 pages of paper and a two gigabyte data stick.

"Too much information—condense it further—you know who I report to," replied the manager with a wave of his hand.

"OK, the misinformation started with CNN at 11:47, and spread to the other major networks within nine minutes. The images were taken from their driver's licenses – no real lead there, but the video was more of a challenge, we were able to analyze and match the number of pixels and refresh rate to come up with makes and models and then track back to suppliers, you know with the exchange rate with world currency the US dollar actually…"

"The point, get to what we need to know," interrupted the manager while closing the three ring binder. The reporting leader paused and then continued.

"Some of the video came from cameras mounted in the vehicles—the vehicles that were blown up!" The manager took a deep breath and continued, "Some came from the police's own vehicle dash cams."

"This was really very well done, nice production quality, great timing and well prepared—who ever put out this information is well connected, efficient and thorough—all in all a very impressive mis- information campaign."

The manager was very proud of the team and went on to add, "The team even put their notes on the bottom of the presentation so you can see the details and how we came to the conclusions." The Director was already down the hall when he yelled over his shoulder, "Well done, thank you."

Chapter 29

Washington, DC, Project Hotel Sierra

Deputy Director, we are reviewing the report from Media Monitoring now and can confirm a strong likely hood that Homeland Security is the source of the bogus information," reported the manager eagerly.

Silence from the Deputy Director.

"Sir? I know it isn't a 100% but…" added the manager hesitantly.

"Look, we need facts and evidence. Keep digging," he commanded.

"Ok, we were looking for a home run but I think we have a bunch of bunt singles," the manager continued.

"The vehicles were bought with funds through a catering company to a holding company from the Homeland Security employee entertainment budget. The men were all subcontractors through a company similar to Blackwater – we are digging for more on them. An odd coincidence is that all of the men killed in the vehicle explosions in Pierre changed their names in the last four years."

The Deputy Director lectured the manager, "You know there are no coincidences."

"We are working on a full background on all of those guys and tracking their communication," said the manager.

The Deputy Director thanked the manager and as he walked back to his office he stopped by the field office Command center.   As he walked into the reception area people recognized him.

"Yes, Deputy Director, how can I help you?" asked the receptionist.

"I need information on our field office in South Dakota," he said.

"I will bring you to the Area Director, follow me." The receptionist said as she jumped up and motioned for him to follow.

In the office of the Area Field Manager, the Deputy Director demanded, "Tell me everything you know about our South Dakota office."

Chapter 30

Sioux Falls, South Dakota

Elliot Ray was the youngest state FBI field office manager at 29 years old and he was embarrassed by this field office. The office looked shabby, the field agents and analysts dressed like they bought their clothes at Goodwill, and there was almost no attention to policy and procedures.

Field Office Manager Elliot Ray wore a suit everyday, he worked out, ate healthy food, didn't smoke or drink and he read real books, not just magazines and internet stories.

His hair was dark black and very tightly curled hair that he kept cut very short. He was not tall, and a bit stocky, strong arms and hands. He was young but was a great listener and observer. He was normally quiet unless he needed to make an impression.

He completed his undergraduate degree in Computer Science at age 20 because he completed two years of college while still in high school.

He joined the Marines after college because he wanted to learn how to fly helicopters. He earned his private pilots license at age 17 but didn't fly much because he could not afford to rent a plane. He wanted to fly the Apache or Cobra attack helicopters but was washed out during training. He ended up as co-pilot on the Blackhawk helicopter, transporting troops and injured in Iraq after training in the United States.

He completed his tour of duty and returned right into the FBI.

He was not shy about wanting to be promoted and he was always looking for opportunities to learn and grow.

*   *   *   *

He was back in the FBI Field Office on a Saturday because he received a call from Dean Breckinridge saying they had a visitor and it was an emergency, come immediately.

As he entered the office Agent Elliot Ray said, "What is the emergency, Agent Breckinridge?"

"Aw, call me Beano, Chief," whined Agent Breckinridge. Agent Dean Breckinridge dressed like the TV Detective McCloud from the 70's television show. He wore cowboy boots, was tall and tanned, had a big bushy mustache and was way too friendly and outgoing for Agent Ray's taste. His style grated on Elliot, because he refused to follow policy and procedure, he was a true cowboy; a maverick.

"Chief, we have a visitor from the Pierre Police Department," said Beano as he pointed to a police officer with a dirty face, a tear in the knee of his pants and holding his hat in his hands.

"Pierre!" Elliot exclaimed, "Agent Breckinridge, thanks for calling me."

"They call me Buck," the officer said and held out his hand. "Would you like some coffee or a drink?" Elliot asked while pointing to a chair at the conference table. "What can we do for you?"

"We gotta helluva mess here and we need your help," Officer Buck pleaded as he reached for the cup of coffee. "The media reports are wrong, dead wrong. We got a good department; there is no corruption, we are clean, there is something going on that's big, real big," Buck explained speaking quickly between sips of the coffee.

Elliott's personal cell phone rang, he looked at the number and held up his hand and answered the phone, "Field Manager Elliot Ray here." The Deputy Director was calling from the Area Field Managers Office, "I am here with your manager and we have an update and a request."

"I am listening sir," Elliot said while walking to a private office.
"There is a situation in Pierre, we need someone on the ground to offer assistance and gather information," the Deputy Director said. Elliot had never talked with someone so high up in the chain of command.

"We can do that sir—we have an interesting visitor here, from Pierre."

They set up a video conference with Agent Breckinridge, Manager Elliot and Officer Buck in Sioux Falls to meet with the Deputy Director and the Area Field Office Manager from their office in Washington DC. They reviewed everything, listening to Buck's story with few interruptions, and few additional questions. The Deputy Director recorded the conference and forwarded it to the Media Monitoring group and the Hotel Sierra Project.

After Buck told them everything he could remember, the Deputy Director said, "OK Elliot, get your crew over there and help out—monitor the situation and protect the local law enforcement officers. We believe the media reports are false, so don't let anyone do anything with those good officers!"

"Yes sir. Pierre is about three hours away by car," Elliot responded.

"Elliot, we have another mission for you, you need to stay in Sioux Falls, but there's no time to waste, get rolling!" the Deputy Director commanded.

"Elliot -- please stay on the line—we need to talk privately." he added.

Buck and Beano exited the conference room; Elliot slowly closed the door and gently sat down.

"Elliot, you have extensive knowledge of Salt Lake City because you were stationed there two years working at the field office. Your mission is to get to Salt Lake City, monitor the Church of Latter Day Saints communication center and await further instructions."

Elliot was disappointed he would not be going to Pierre but excited about the new mission. He was an expert in audio and video surveillance. He was promoted to Field Office Manager because of his exceptional work performance—he has the reputation of and an excellent officer, creative and a bulldog, very patient and a tremendous planner. He looked forward to the mission. He liked to build electronic equipment and interesting gadgets from common items in his spare time.

"I'm ready and will go immediately," he said.

"Be aware you need to get there without taking commercial flights and don't use your credit card and stay away from surveillance cameras," the Deputy Director warned. "We will inform the Salt Lake City Team you are on your way; let us know when you are in place," he continued.

After the conference call Elliot joined Buck and Beano in the reception area. Buck gave Galen's personal cell phone number to Elliot, "You should call Galen to get more inside information," he told him trying to be helpful.

Elliot didn't want to call Galen, he had a mission and thought talking to the Pierre Police Chief would just delay his mission but, at Buck and Beano's encouragement he made the call.

"Here, use my cell phone, he will recognize my number and talk to you right away," Buck offered. Elliot took the phone and called Galen.

*   *   *   *   *   *   *

Galen and Jerry were in the plane on their way to Rochester Minnesota. Near the Minnesota and South Dakota border, Galen's phone rang; he recognized the number as belonging to Buck. The Cessna Skylane had a great intercom system—he could hook his cell phone directly to the plane. He answered the phone, "Hello, Buck, what is the news?"

"Chief Anderson this is Agent Elliot Ray with the FBI, I've just gotten a detailed briefing from your officer Buck, he is a good man."

"We need help, this is big and the media reports are bullshit!" Galen shouted. Elliot recognized the background noise and asked, "Where are you?" Galen lied and said, "The windows on my car are blown out –that's just wind noise. I can pull over if needed"

Galen then told the truth, "We need evidence and we are on the way to Rochester to stop one of the sabotage missions."

"This is not a job for local authorities, leave this to the FBI, we can handle this—it's out of your jurisdiction, come in," Elliot pleaded. He recognized the drone from an airplane—he knew they were in the air and —at that point; he put the story together and challenged Galen.

"You and Jerry stole a plane and you are on the run and on your way to stop this conspiracy, come in, leave this to us."

Jerry reduced power to idle and pointed the nose down to try to maintain a safe speed and reduce the noise so they would not be discovered and intercepted. They knew they would not be able clear themselves if they are in jail, the evidence looked overwhelming so they had to continue with their plan.

Galen then said, "Agent Ray, we are going through with this. We will call you when we have the evidence." Galen and Jerry nodded in agreement and then he hung up.

Elliot had a new plan to get to Salt Lake City.

Chapter 31

Pierre, South Dakota

The Police station was surrounded by Homeland Security and TSA officers. The parking lot was blocked and the street in front of the station was also blocked off with barricades. Inside a tense standoff continued.

There were two Homeland Security agents for each local police officer and staff person at the station. The exits were blocked and the only Homeland Security person in a suit asked, "Where is the Police Chief?" Everyone answered the same, "Last I heard, he went out to Bob's place to help search for evidence."

They tried to be helpful adding, "Have you looked out there?"

"Have you found his truck?"

"It's Saturday afternoon, have you checked his place?"

"Sometimes he goes fishing on Saturday afternoons" and

"Maybe we should go look for him."

The Homeland Security suit was very frustrated and perturbed when he shouted, "No one is going anywhere, you had your chance to participate. You are all considered accessories to the conspiracy and are all under arrest—move them all to holding!" The guy in the suit pointed to the cell block and motioned for the technicians to occupy each work station. They begin reviewing files and notes looking for evidence that didn't exist. The Homeland Security officers herded the Pierre Police officers into the holding cells as they grumbled and shuffled their feet.

*   *   *   *   *   *   *

The Crime Lab technicians were working in a temporary facility processing the destroyed trucks like bees on wild flowers. They were still working on the evidence, they reported to the Attorney General who turned the reports over to the FBI and Homeland Security.

At the South Dakota Justice building, Homeland Security was at the office of the Assistant Attorney General. The Assistant Attorney General knew what they wanted. He figured Galen's phone was being monitored and now he was involved. He didn't go home for supper that day.

Chapter 32

Salt Lake City, Utah

M adam Leader called her contact in the police department. "Thanks for the photos from your cameras, very helpful. I have just one more request." She spoke in a soft, seductive, gentle voice that made people who know her shiver.

"Excuse me for being skeptical about this being your last request," said the frustrated man on the phone. "Oh relax," she purred, "you can trust me with your secret – you see, we both have something to hide – we are the perfect partners."

"You seem to be the beneficiary of other's misfortunes," the man said trying not to offend her.

"Are you asking for money?" she asked. "I can give you money, but that means a bigger, longer commitment. What kind of man are you?"

"I'm a man who has limits and I'm almost paid up."

"Ah yes, a moral man are you. You think that by paying back the money you embezzled, you would be even? Ha, now the cover-up and deception are bigger than the crime, but I forgive you. I know you are a good man." She spoke like a snake hissing, then continued.

"Follow Jerry Sherwood, let us know what he knows; your secret is safe with me." She finished her call by saying,

"Don't let me down. You, of all people, know what I do when I am disappointed." She disconnected the line and went back to watching the monitors in her darkened office.

She called her team into her office. "We need something on our friends at the FBI – who has something, anything, we can use?

"I have an agent in Atlanta that was arrested for domestic violence," one team member offered.

"Boring."

"I have another who lied on their resume" said another team member.

"Oh please, is that all you have,"

"I know an agent that is researching sex change operations" said a third team member.

"Better, but not good enough. Run their credit reports and look for agents in dire straits, look for cash flow to prostitutes, look for correlations with drug and mob leaders, club memberships, arts and entertainment tickets. Come on people, be creative. You were hired for your brains, not your good looks so start using your heads. I need something in 60 minutes – I'll be in my office," she barked. They noticed she didn't say, "Any questions?" She never ended a meeting with the statement, "Any questions?" And no one ever asked a question.

She shooed them out, lowered the power blinds and went back to her monitors.

Chapter 33

3,000 Feet Above Ground Level, Eastern South Dakota.

Jerry set the auto pilot on the Cessna Skylane to maintain altitude and heading. They did not turn on the GPS. They knew the GPS sent a signal as it received signals and could be tracked. They used old technology – radio navigation. The radio received transmissions from ground - based antenna usually at or near airports. The pilot would monitor the dial on the instrument panel to stay on course. As the pilot approached one site they could either track as they are moving away or they could dial in the frequency of the next antenna.

"This plane seems fast," Galen said, "How fast are we going?"

"We have a little tailwind so we are going about 170 miles per hour," Jerry said after checking his watch and timing his checkpoints. "We should get to Rochester right at dusk," Jerry added. Galen then said, "We need the evidence—we don't need to stop them. We can get a lockdown and quarantine later."

"What's the plan once we get to the plant?" Jerry asked.

"We gotta get there first. How do we get from the airport to the plant?" Galen asked.

"Not a problem, we stop at the Fixed Base Operator (FBO), get fuel, rent a hangar space, and they will have a courtesy car for us to use." Jerry happily announced.

"Just follow my lead when we get there." Jerry smiled and winked.

About 30 miles out from the Rochester airport, Jerry radioed the air traffic controller for permission and directions to land. It was a very quiet night, they were directed straight in. On the ground they asked for directions to the FBO and taxied directly there. There was a skinny young man in a worn jumpsuit who jumped out of the office and waved them to the fuel pump.

Jerry shut down the engine, went through the post flight checklist and then hopped out and said, "Please fill'er up; can we rent a hangar for the night?" The young man grabbed his wooden ladder and pulled the hose to the wing tanks and said, "Sure thing."

Jerry and Galen did a post flight inspection of the plane and Jerry asked, "How much for the hangar over night?"

"Twenty bucks for you, because you bought fuel," said the skinny attendant. "OK, the fuel is $113.85 and $20 for the hangar," he said.

"Wonderful. Do you have a courtesy car so we can go into town? We will be leaving later tonight—are you around to get the plane out when we get back?" Jerry asked with a smile while handing him cash.

"Yeah, I'll be here all night—I'll get your receipt and the keys to the car," the attendant said.

Galen followed Jerry and kept quiet—he recognized he was very conspicuous wearing a Pierre, South Dakota Police Department uniform while they walked to the FBO parking lot.

The airport courtesy car was a mid 90s Dodge Caravan – a blue minivan—they would blend right in. They stopped on the way out of the airport at the terminal and asked for directions to the milk processing plant.

They drove the short distance stopping along the way at a fast food restaurant. By the time they arrived at the milk processing plant it was dark, so they parked across the street about half a block from the shipping and loading dock.

"If I was trying to get in to put bacteria in a milk processing plant, I would arrange for a diversion, enter through the loading dock and wear a disguise," Galen said.

"Wow, you would be a great criminal," Jerry quipped with eyebrows raised.

"You know what they say, there's a fine line between the police and the criminals," Galen said with a smile. He then became somber and said, "Thanks for helping, I couldn't have gotten this far without your help."

"I'm glad to help, we gotta do something to clear our names and get to the bottom of this conspiracy—these Homeland Security guys scare me—they are killers and I don't know what else to do," Jerry said.

"How are you doing? Most people in the department get counseling after a fatal firearm discharge." Galen tested Jerry to see whether he has processed the traumatic events of the day.

"I'm OK, I guess. I do keep seeing the images of Joe Smith – I feel bad he had to die. I wish I didn't even go flying today—if I just stayed home, none of this would have happened."

"It takes a long time to get over what you went through today," Galen offered calmly.

Then Jerry asked, "What's the plan?"

"We wait and watch," said Galen.

*   *   *   *

Minutes later a big sedan with large chrome wheels and tires drove through the parking lot and pulled up to the front door. A finely dressed man and a chunky black woman in a skimpy outfit approached the front door. The door was locked so they started pounding. A janitor heard the noise, saw the people through the door and brought the shift manager to the reception area.

The stripper smiled wide and said, "Heeey, we are here to party!" Through the door the guy said, "Yeah, we got a gig here with a stripper for employees who have birthdays." The shift manager shook his head and said, "No way."

"You're kinda cute, what's your name? I'm already paid for, it'll take about 10 minutes, it'll be fun for everyone," she pleaded while straightening her hair and smiling a coy smile.

"Who paid you?" the shift manager asked.

"All the guys on the shift I guess. If you turn us away there are no refunds," he warned.

Several of the guys noticed the visitor and told each other about the sexy stripper in the lobby. The shift manager went back to the production area and yelled, "Which smart ass arranged for a stripper for somebody's birthday?" There were about 12 guys and they all yelled "YEAH!"

"OK, you bunch of animals, you have 10 minutes— whose birthday is it anyway?" They looked at each other and finally a young guy named Brett and an older guy named Maynard said they had a birthday this month. All the guys hooted and hollered. Someone pulled up two chairs and another went into the office to unplug the monitoring cameras.

The guy accompanying the stripper carried a large boom box CD player and pushed play. Rick James 'Super Freak' blasted out of the speakers and the switch was turned on in the dancer.

She had three inch platform heels and kinda wobbled as she walked—she didn't need to walk much, she wiggled and jiggled and rocked her hips in a seductive walk. Her bikini was not large enough to cover her. Both men received an up close and personal lap dance while Rick James sang about a sweet girl he could never bring home to meet his mother.

All the guys in the whole facility ran to see the show and yelled word of encouragement to the two lucky guys at the center of their attention. They didn't notice a second car with two men move through the plant entrance and park in the employee parking area. The perfect diversion allowed the trespasser to enter the building through the unattended loading dock doors.

He wore white pants, white shirt and a white smock. He also wore white rubber boots, a white hair net and a white hard hat – they had done their homework; he was dressed exactly the same as all the employees. He carried a map of the plant and a piping diagram – he went directly to the output from the pasteurizer and attached a direct feeder through the sampling nipple so the bacteria could be fed into the system. He disguised the feeder so it would not be immediately noticed.

Galen had circled around the plant and had seen the stripper enter the building; he went around the back and got in a position to watch the accomplice and the saboteur.

Jerry's job was to disable the car – he slowly and silently crawled behind the second car. On his back, he slowly inched underneath it carrying a very sharp pocket knife which he used to carefully cut any wires he could find. He was trying to cut the wires to the fuel pump so the car would be immobilized.

The accomplice in the car was the lookout – he didn't notice Jerry or Galen.

Galen stepped out of the shadows of the parking lot lights and followed the guy out of the plant.

The saboteur did not see Galen so he called Madam Leader as he was walking from the plant. "It's done, mission accomplished."

The driver nervously attempted to start the car as he saw his partner return to the get away car. As soon as the saboteur got in the car he said, "Drive!"

The car would not start, the engine turned over but would not fire and run. The driver pushed the pedal down and pumped it, but still the engine did not start.

Galen walked up, still in his Pierre Police uniform and said, "Hey guys, having problems?" He slowed his walk and moved his hand to his weapon when he noticed the passenger reaching for his gun. The passenger looked away then suddenly pulled out his gun, fired when Galen was about 30 feet away. Galen spun and fired two quick shots, one round hit the shooter in the right shoulder as he dove behind a car. Blood spattered on the dome light turned the light pink. The other round went through the back window and it shattered.

Jerry was startled at the gunfire and quickly crawled to the driver's side front door and when the driver opened his door to get out; Jerry took his knife and made a deep cut between the pant leg and the top of his shoes. The driver fell and cried out.

The passenger was distracted by the cry and looked at the driver as Galen jumped up and fired 3 more rapid fire shots—one round hit his chest and the passenger dropped his gun and was dead. The car was filled with gun smoke and fabric dust from the bullets that tore through the upholstery. The door ajar chime was ringing as Jerry crawled on top of the struggling driver.

He had been on the high school wrestling team and knew how to keep a guy down. The driver had a weapon in his hand and was trying to point the weapon at Jerry, so Jerry slammed the guys head twice into the pavement as Galen walked around to the driver's side.

"Way to go, nice job. Is he dead?" Galen asked.

"Nope – it's probably better that he is alive; let's handcuff him and call the police," Jerry said with his hands shaking.

Galen was lifting him back into the car when Jerry said, "Not the steering wheel, too many resources –he could escape, I got a better idea." Jerry laid him back on the ground by the front wheel and put one arm around the tire and the other in front of the tire and hooked the handcuffs tightly on his wrists and proudly remarked,

"He'll have to chew his arms off, drive the car over his arms or lift the car to get away."

"Nice, let's get out of here," Galen said.

"Whoa, we need stuff they have," Jerry said while searching through the driver's billfold, he grabbed several hundred dollars and his cell phone. Then he grabbed the gun held it up and smiled at Galen.

"Wait a minute Jerry," Galen said, "I don't think it's a good idea for you to have a gun. Have you ever owned a gun?"

"No, but I have fired a gun, twice, and I killed a man – I am qualified. By the way, where is the safety on this thing?" Jerry replied while twisting the pistol in his hand. Galen rolled his eyes and said, "Yeah sure, good idea."

Galen went through the passenger's billfold, took money, his weapon, and extra ammo clips. He popped the trunk and rummaged through the gear there. He picked out radios, percussion grenades and smoke bombs. They saw the stripper leave and ducked so they would not be seen.

"We gotta get out of here," Jerry whispered.

"OK, call 911 from their phone," schemed Galen.

They ran to the courtesy car after calling 911 and drove directly back to the airport. On the way Galen called back the FBI Manager in Sioux Falls.

"We were successful, all the evidence you need is at the milk processing plant near Rochester. There is one dead and one alive -- their ID's are there. We have notified the local authorities, I suggest you quarantine the plant and find out where the other planes went with the bacteria," Galen spoke with intensity as a result of the adrenaline.

"Thanks a lot guys, but it's time to come in, we can finish this," Elliot said.

"I don't think so, we don't believe you can help. We gave you the information and the FBI has not done a damn thing right -- we are going to Salt Lake City to finish this," Galen said with authority.

"And do what? Go where? Confront who?" Elliot teased. "Your team in Pierre are under arrest—they need you, leave this to the professionals," Elliot added. Galen reluctantly said, "We don't believe you can solve this problem—we must go and we will be successful. Goodbye."

"Wait, wait! don't hang up."

"Galen", Elliot continued, "I think I can help, I think I _have_ to help," Elliot was thinking on the fly.

"Take me with you, I worked in Salt Lake City, I know the people and the resources, I am a surveillance expert. I am on the way, I can help get the equipment you need and a place to rest – you can't fly all night."

Galen was thinking. Jerry heard one side of the conversation while he was driving back to the airport and he was confused.

"They have my parents!" Elliot blurted out on the phone to Galen. "Those bastards have kidnapped my parents and want me to tank the investigation. I gotta get there and fix this without them knowing—you guys have a good chance and I can help. I'm going to go without you if I have to. Meet me at the Tea, South Dakota airport in about two hours." Elliot finished.

"We'll think about it." Galen said before ending the call. He then filled in the other side of their conversation and the offer from Elliot the FBI agent.

They did another preflight, checked the fuel and warmed up the engine. They checked the current weather conditions, received clearance from the control tower and were given permission to depart immediately.

"We need to decide what we are going to do," Jerry said.

"Can we trust him?"

"We have to – this is a big conspiracy and if the FBI cannot help, who can?" Galen said. "We are on our own here." After a pause he said, "Let's go to Tea."

Jerry was full of energy when they took off but after about an hour he was starting to droop. The Skylane is a wonderful plane—fast comfortable and it handles great. The air was smooth, as it usually is at night. The lights were mesmerizing. With the drone of the engine and a quiet Galen, Jerry could not get the image of Joe in his plane off his mind. He could see Joe's bloody arm caught in the seat belt hanging out the door.

He blinked his eyes and stared at the glow of city lights from Sioux Falls when he was 75 miles away. The Tea, South Dakota airport is just outside the city and the Sioux Falls airport airspace. It is a small, quiet airport where they would be able to get in, meet Elliot, rest a bit and get on their way.

Chapter 34

Salt Lake City, Utah

C ongratulations Madam Leader, what a successful operation, no one can stop us. All the other plans are in place. We have the milk plants ready, our lobbyists are ready, the media is prepared and all our contacts are ready for their duties," the young woman said with a wide smile.

"I've read the reports and seen the video, you need to be respectful of all the assets we lost today." Madam Leader barked. "We still have the loose ends in South Dakota, what is the status of that mess?"

"Well…" the young woman said.

"Well is not an answer," interrupted Madam Leader. Regaining some composure, the young woman who took over the operation continued to explain, "The evidence is disposed of, all information trails have been eliminated and there are absolutely no money trails to follow. Doing all those computer models to prepare has allowed us to deliver on budget and within the parameters set out in the original plan."

"Yeah, yeah, real nice, but you still have some loose ends, that bastard who killed Joey knows way too much and he has been too resourceful to live. Get it done and don't screw this up," Madam Leader demanded. The younger woman closed her brief and turned away. "I won't screw up Mom, I need to see that Jerry dead too."

Mary Rose was the sister of Joe Smith and the daughter of Madam Leader. She worked for the Leadership Council like her mother and her great aunt. She was working to build her power and sustain her position in the Leadership Council. She patiently worked to maintain her contacts and be connected to others with power.

This was a great opportunity to assert her skills and dedication to the church.

Chapter 35

Washington DC FBI Headquarters

T he Media Monitoring report was forwarded to the Hotel Sierra project team. They assembled all the information regarding the alleged conspiracy but it was late in the day and they were losing energy. The team was following the evidence they had, the vehicles destroyed in fires, the men in the trucks, and staffing of Homeland Security and TSA employees.

Project Hotel Sierra contacted the South Dakota Crime lab proactively for an update on their information gathering. The conspirators had a deep communication network – how were they communicating with the field? Where was their headquarters? How could they track or intercept these conspirators?

The manager kept challenging the analysts and researchers. "Keep digging, consider every possibility, no matter how crazy and improbable, we must check it out."

"What if they had their own satellite?" one analyst mentioned. "Does anyone know if Homeland Security has their own satellite?" the manager yelled.

"I'm on it," another researcher said and his fingers made a higher pitch clacking on the keyboard. "I'll look at contractor records and payloads and I will check on international orbital payloads."

*   *   *   *

The Mormon Conspiracy

The Media Monitoring team noticed a ground swell of small market media and internet based news outlets telling a different story – a story more in line with the original story told by Jerry Sherwood. The source is a network of aviation email lists and the local media members that were at the initial news conference. They were doing ground work in South Dakota to verify and support the story.

The Deputy Director pulled together a team to work on this alleged conspiracy and provide support for the field. The team was looking for the destinations of the bacteria deliveries, cross referencing flights, milk plants and Mormons. One interesting thing, they found 25% of fresh grade A milk bottling facilities are Mormon owned. The FBI believed the motivation might be industrial espionage – cause problems for other milk producers to weaken them and strengthen their own position.

The other question on the Deputy Directors' mind was 'How the Mormons would benefit from the chaos likely to occur with the interruption to the food chain?'

He asked the team to continue looking at the relationship between the Church of Latter Day Saints and Homeland Security. They would have something to move on if they could find a solid connection. There was an unspoken sense of urgency – they were peeling back layers of this conspiracy like layers of an onion and the results scared even seasoned FBI associates.

Chapter 36

Rochester, Minnesota

The local police were already responding to a citizen report of gunshots near the milk processing plant when they got a 911 call from someone who provided more detailed reports.

The first cruiser arrived and immediately called for back-up, and an ambulance. The officer set up a perimeter and started tending to the man handcuffed to the front wheel. The guy in the car was dead but the other person was alive. Two other squad cars arrived and the first officer went into the plant to see if there were any witnesses and get someone to identify the worker. The guy in the passenger seat was still wearing the white clothes that made him look like a plant worker.

The shift manager went red in the face when the police officer showed up at the locked front door. His hands were shaking as he unlocked the front door. "Yes, officer, can we help you?"

The officer asked in the unflappable flat affect voice, "Did anything unusual happen tonight?" The manager stammered, "No, nothing unusual. Why?"
"Well, there was a shooting in your parking lot and I think one of your employees is dead – could you come with me to identify the body?" the officer asked waving his arm towards the door.

They walked out and around to the back, the shift manager slowed his walk as he got closer to the car and gasped when he saw the dead man in the front seat.   He moved closer as the officer shined the light on the face of the dead man. He finally said, "He ain't one of mine."

"Maybe a guy from an earlier shift?" the officer pressed moving his flashlight closer to the dead mans face.

"Nope, he don't have the ID badge and I know all the guys on the other shifts—I've worked here 17 years, I know everyone and he don't work here."

"What's going on here officer?" The plant manager was backing away.

"You better check to see if anything is missing, and don't talk to the media," warned the officer as he pulled out his small notebook.   "I also want the names of everyone working tonight."

An ambulance, tow truck and a black SUV pulled in together and drove right through the yellow crime scene tape. The EMTs rushed to the man who was down, four men got out of the SUV, two brought a body bag for the dead man and one went to talk with the first officer.

"Good evening officer," he said flashing a Homeland Security badge. "How can we assist you?"

"I think we are supposed to leave the dead man there until the coroner comes out, and this is a crime scene, you probably shouldn't have driven right through here," the officer said tentatively.

The EMT's worked very quickly and moved the injured man to the ambulance and the dead man was put in a body bag and then into the ambulance which sped out—but without sirens and lights.

One of the other officers yelled, "Hey, you can't take that body!" While the officers chased after the ambulance and then complained to the Homeland Security guys, the tow truck backed up and quickly pulled the car onto the flatbed. The officers were now yelling even louder, "This is our crime scene, you can't take that car – this is evidence!" The first officer ran to his car and called in the need for back up and reported Homeland Security was interfering with the investigation.

The remaining Homeland security officers were picking up evidence, bagging it and stashing it in the SUV. They sprayed the blood on the ground with ammonia while one of them talked with the officers.

"We are just trying to help out, of course this is your crime scene, you can always talk with me later or your chief can talk with our commander."

"But, you can't take the car too," insisted the lead officer. "We will set up a hotline for you and we have all the materials at our warehouse and lab in Minneapolis."

The Homeland Security agent said, "It's been a pleasure to work with you, so nice. We better get going, call anytime, really." He yelled as he was getting in the final departing SUV.

In a flash the crime scene was clean; the local police officers were stunned—the Homeland Security officers ignored them and left before their boss arrived.

"What just happened?" asked the first officer.
"Who called them?" the second officer asked.
"Where did they take everything?" asked the third.

Chapter 37

Pierre, South Dakota Crime Lab

The technicians were working as fast as they could, tow trucks kept bringing more SUV carcasses and charred remains of bodies were backed up. They called for a refrigerated truck because the morgue was full.

On a counter in a labeled paper bag were the clothes worn by Jerry Sherwood after he shot the kidnapper in his plane. The shirts and pants are splattered with blood, brain matter and tiny body parts of the kidnapper. They had been so focused on the bigger trucks and multiple bodies they forgot about the shirt.

One of the technicians remembered the shirt and started processing the blood and materials to gather a specimen for a DNA analysis. There was a stack of specimens that were ready to be sent to the state lab in Sioux Falls.

Galen had called the State Patrol earlier to arrange use of their plane to transport the specimens to the lab. The trooper hand delivered all the sealed containers from Pierre directly to the lab—naturally these items were the highest priority – the trip would take about an hour by plane, they would have the results in four to six hours.

They heard the local police chief was missing and the police station had been taken over by Homeland Security. They had been sending all updates to the FBI and Homeland Security – they had not heard from the local police for hours. Funny thing though, is that no TSA or Homeland Security agent is assisting or even asking for information.

*   *   *   *

FBI agent Elliot Ray hung up the phone after hearing an update from Galen and Jerry – they had successfully caught the guys who tried to sabotage the milk plant in Rochester. Elliot called the Deputy Director with the news.

"Sorry to call so late but I knew you would want to know about the conspiracy." He told him about what Jerry and Galen have accomplished.

"Here's the kicker, they're going to Salt Lake City to get to the bottom of the conspiracy and I want to go with them. I can monitor their efforts and stop them from doing something stupid," Elliot explained.

The Deputy Director recognized opportunity when he saw it. "OK, good idea, take what you need. We have been digging; we do not have the locations of the other milk plants, yet."

"We believe there is a mole in the police department – it could be Galen. We also have more and more evidence of a Mormon connection – we believe there is something bigger than just bacteria in milk behind this. Be careful."

"I can handle this – it's good to be going back to Salt Lake City and good to be in the field again," replied Elliot. "I also need a back story – I told them my parents were kidnapped by Homeland Security ordered by the Mormon Church."

"Not a problem, we can cover that," the Deputy Director said. "And we will have DNA identification of the guy killed in the plane and the guys in the SUVs soon, stay in touch with me."

FBI Field Office Manager Elliot Ray started packing. He selected weapons and ammo, grenades, explosives and timers. He also packed all his AV gear – he had been building switches and surveillance gear. Elliot has a talent for designing and modifying electronic gear to suit his needs. He has some new gadgets that have not been field tested. His idea for the mission would require a small team.

Chapter 38
Tea Airport near Sioux Falls, South Dakota

G alen and Jerry had a smooth flight – it was a clear night
and the winds had died down. The trip from Rochester,
Minnesota to Sioux Falls, South Dakota was an easy
flight – almost the whole flight follows Interstate 90 across
southern Minnesota. The lights were pretty, each farmstead had
a yard light, and cities were spread out connected by roads
traveled by cars with white and red lights.

They had to travel south around the airspace for the big
airport at Sioux Falls and they landed without incident. Jerry
was getting tired – what a day. In one day he had flown from
Pierre to Canada and back again then a trip to Rochester and now
back to Tea, South Dakota.

"I'm going to take a nap while we wait for the FBI guy,"
Jerry said noticeably tired. Galen was too nervous to sleep, so he
stayed awake and kept watch.

Within 15 minutes Elliot arrived, lights off driving very
slowly. Galen had hidden around the corner of a hangar when
he saw the car slowly approaching. Elliot shone a flashlight on
his badge and walked forward to the darkened plane. Galen
walked up behind him and said, "What's the name of the officer
who you met recently? Don't turn around!"

"Buck," Elliot answered without any quick movements.
"OK, keep it down, Jerry is sleeping."
"So you are from the FBI, I don't understand why you
don't just tell your buddies at the Bureau to get off their asses

and bust this conspiracy." Galen was shaking with excitement and anger.

"People like you think we can do anything – there are limits and sometimes the enemy will sacrifice almost everything if their larger goals can be reached. There is more to this conspiracy than we know," Agent Ray said, hoping, Galen would accept his excuse for coming along.

"You better pull your weight, sometimes you gotta take control and do it yourself." Galen was worked up and tired and ready to do or say something he shouldn't. He turned and walked back to the plane.

Elliot wondered what he had gotten himself into. What a way to start a mission.

Chapter 39
Pierre, South Dakota

The Pierre Police department officers and staff were all in the temporary lockup at the police station under the watchful eyes of the FBI.

The FBI agents from the Sioux Falls field office entered the station laughing and talking loud. FBI Agent Dean Breckinridge carried a big bag of donuts and the other three agents carried coffee and bags of candy.

Agent Breckinridge yelled with a smile, "Hello Homeland Security. We are your humble servants from the Sioux Falls FBI Field office. You gotta call me Beano, OK?"

"My friendly associates are passing around some treats – that's the way we take care of our friends," continued Agent Beano Breckinridge. As the other FBI agents were handing out the treats, one went back to the lock up area and searched for keys. With some instruction from the Pierre officers, he found the key and unlocked their doors and led them out.

The Homeland Security officers pulled out their handguns when they saw the escaped Pierre police officers. Beano held his hands down to calm his team and the Pierre police officers.

"Look guys, these folks need to do their jobs, they know the people, they know the city. These are dedicated, loyal Americans who have pledged to fight injustice, protect the citizens and serve their fellow Pierre, South Dakota neighbors," Beano said sincerely and then ended his speech with a smile.

"Yeah, very funny, this is a neat trick, ha ha," the Homeland Security guy in a suit said with fake sincerity.

"These officers are our prisoners under the authority of the President of the United States. Thanks for the goodies but you all are about 30 seconds from joining them in the lock up," he said as he waved his arms and pointed at each of the FBI agents.

Beano didn't break his big smile, "Welcome to South Dakota, wouldn't it make more sense just to let these guys work and watch them—you out number us poor country folks two to one? Exactly what have you boys done to gather evidence, and find who is responsible for these deaths of these fine young men?"

Beano continued like a poker player who could be bluffing. "You boys are 15 seconds from a public relations nightmare. How would this look on the six o'clock news: *'Unarmed small town cops shot in their police station by Homeland Security,'*" he said in his fake TV announcer voice.

Beano waved his arm in a welcoming gesture to the Pierre police officers and gave his biggest - friendliest - South Dakota smile.

The Homeland Security suit made a hand gesture and his agents lowered their weapons and put them into their holsters. He put a big insincere smile on his face, put his arm around Agent Breckinridge and quietly said, "Agent Breckinridge." "Call me Beano," interrupted Agent Breckinridge with another big smile.

"Agent Breckinridge, Beano, you and your team have 30 minutes to produce some results – and all communication goes through me," the guy in the suit said as he pointed his finger at Beano trying to sound threatening.

Beano quickly said, "You got it, Chief. All results go to Homeland Security and the FBI." He turned to the staff and demanded, "Come on guys, we are all working together, find out who these guys who died in the SUVs were, where is this Bob guy, where did the planes go, what are the potential targets and where is a good place for barbeque in Pierre!"

All the Pierre police officers and even the FBI agents were smiling when the Homeland Security leader stomped into the Chief's office, slammed the door and made a call to Washington DC.

In Chief Galen Anderson's office the Homeland Security Chief called his Superior. "This is embarrassing, getting upstaged by these hicks, it is unprofessional. Don't they have any respect?"

"Shut up and quit your whining, you deserve everything you are getting. You have to earn their respect," the Homeland Security Director said.

"What do we know about this conspiracy, what are we as an agency doing to find who killed those men? Our men," he said under his breath.

"Remember your place, Agent. You represent Homeland Security, remember who you serve."

"There is mounting evidence the last two are Homeland Security employees and the others are subcontractors. There is undeniable evidence that they were killed in explosions and fires set remotely." The Lead Agent questioned his superior.

"Insubordination is not what I expect from you, consider your career, watch what you say and do," the Director snarled. "Homeland Security is not run like the local quilting club – this is not a Democracy. You are hired to follow orders. I suggest you do that."

The Lead Agent hung up the phone and put his head in his hands. What was going on here – why were his leaders stalling and actually preventing him – preventing everyone from solving this mystery?

Chapter 40
Tea, South Dakota Airport

Jerry was just waking up in the front seat of the plane he borrowed from the conspirator Bob near Pierre. He heard voices and woke up groggy—it took a couple of minutes to realize where he was. It was still dark and he was disoriented.

Before he woke up he was dreaming of fixing his house—picking up wood and siding pieces and trying to fit them together like a jig saw puzzle. Not a pleasant dream, wandering around his yard, walking through the debris from the blown up house. In his dream he was yelling at everyone, asking for help to pick up the debris and put the puzzle pieces together. He saw a bloody hand in the rubble and yelled for help. He moved some boards and plaster and insulation to reveal a whole arm covered in blood. He reached for it and then he realized the hand and arm belonged to Joe Smith the kidnapper he shot in his plane. He jerked awake with a gasp. It took him a minute to remember where he was.

Galen brought Elliot around to the front of the plane to meet Jerry. "Jerry, this is the FBI guy I've been talking to," Galen announced.

Elliot held out his hand to Jerry and said, "Elliot Ray here, I've heard a lot about you – pretty impressive!"

"Well, it's too bad about your parents too," Jerry said referring to the story that Elliot's parents had been kidnapped.

"Yeah, those bastards – they even called me to taunt me. I know the FBI is going to be successful in finding my parents and bringing those assholes to justice," Elliot answered.

It was still dark out as the guys talked holding flashlights illuminating each others faces.

"What time is it?" asked Jerry with a jerk.
"Almost five AM," replied Galen as he was looking through the gear Elliot brought and loading the bags into the plane.

"We should get moving—I would like to be wheels up before sunrise," said Jerry as he tucked his shirt in his pants. Jerry got his flashlight and started the preflight inspection.

"Get this gear on board and try to do an inventory of what we have here – we need a plan." Jerry said as he checked the elevator and rudder.

Galen finished loading the gear and said, "We can't use our credit cards for fuel and there is no one here to take our cash, will we need to stop again for fuel or can we make it all the way?"
"No, we'll have to stop half way to re-fuel and take a break – it's almost six hours and the last bit is mountain flying." Jerry said while he was fastening his seat belt.

As Elliot climbed in the back seat and Galen got in the right seat Jerry asked Elliot, "Have you ever flown in a small plane before?"

"I flew helicopters in Iraq for the Marines before I joined the FBI," Elliot announced proudly.

Jerry looked at Galen and pointed to the back seat, "Galen, you're back there and you, you're up here," he said pointing at Elliot while smiling.

"Are you current? How are you with sectionals and navigation?"

"I am not current. I haven't flown as pilot in command for two years. My medical is still good but it's been even longer since I flew one of these," Elliot explained while he patted the instrument panel.

"Let's get rolling; we have been sitting long enough," Galen urged.

"OK Chief," Jerry said, then he yelled, "Clear" and started the engine. After the engine was warmed up and the magneto check, they taxied to the end of the runway, turned on all the flight lights and gave full power. As they were rolling Jerry asked, "I've never seen lights like that...?" as he was looking at flashes of light coming from the far end of the runway.

Elliot saw the flashes and knew immediately –
"Those are gunfire flashes, we are being shot at, evasive maneuvers, NOW!"

Jerry's options were limited as they were headed straight towards the flashes. They were barely fast enough to take off and couldn't turn around. Firing back was not possible.

Jerry switched off the landing light, strobe light and position lights and made a gentle turn at less than 100 feet off the ground. The time from liftoff to when they are high enough to see lights from street lights and the city was the most dangerous time of night flight. The pilot must watch the artificial horizon and fly from instruments in the panel, not what was visible through the windshield.

The flashes continued from two, maybe three locations. Galen and Elliot watched the flashes out the side window in silence. Jerry made a gentle left hand turn barely over a row of hangars. He kept the nose low to build speed.

"BOOM!" They heard a loud boom that sounded like a sledge hammer hitting aluminum skin of the plane. Everyone jumped at the noise. Galen reached down and felt the wind through a hole in the floor, then felt the roof and noticed the exit point for the round. He was lucky, they all were lucky. At least one bullet entered the plane and passed right through.

"Is everybody OK," Elliot asked looking around the cabin. Jerry was busy flying the plane—he lowered the nose and kept it at full power to get to top speed as fast as possible and made some gentle random evasive turns.
"I'm OK," Galen quickly replied.

Jerry watched the fuel levels—if a wing tank had a hole in it, they would see the fuel level decreasing. He also scanned the instruments to look for any other signs of damage – everything looked OK, for now.

Jerry said, "I have an idea – that was too close – we need to send them on a wild goose chase."

He turned to a northern heading. He planned to fly through the Class C airspace around the Sioux Falls airport without permission. The air traffic controllers would notice, make calls and report the infraction.

"Then we'll descend below their radar and turn southwest and get out of here." He turned on the radio to the tower frequency and listened to hear when they showed up on radar.

"You know our transponder is off," Elliot said.

"Yep, we want to avoid being spotted and tracked," Jerry said.

Galen added, "No cell phones, no credit cards and no GPS either. Homeland Security can monitor just about every form of communication except smoke signals and Morse code."

Jerry descended to 800 feet above ground and turned gently southwest after he heard the air traffic controllers notice them and report their course as northbound. A few more miles and he could turn on the strobe and position lights again and climb to normal cruise altitude.

Chapter 41
Washington, DC
FBI Headquarters

B lake had worked for the FBI for almost two years—he was recruited right out of college because of his successful work with legal hacking and security system testing. While in college, companies hired him to try to break into their networks. He was successful most of the time which was good for the company he worked for because they then sold network security systems.

He was recruited right out of college – he thought he had to go through boot camp but for the job he was offered, no boot camp was needed.

At the FBI he got to dress in casual clothes and work on interesting projects. He had started working on getting into the Church of Latter Day Saints Genealogy database months ago. Hacking that database was fun because the programmers who built and maintained the network and database were untrained but creative. They made the network and database extremely difficult to work with for their staff but also very difficult to get into.

He was working on it between other projects, but when he heard of Mormons and the conspiracy, he dedicated himself completely to getting into that database.

It looked like the builders made constant modifications, additions and false files to confuse, disguise and prevent hackers from getting in. Blake liked challenges and he liked the fact that they used common tools in very unorthodox manner.

He was on the verge of getting in. When he got in he planned copy files and get out quickly and quietly.

Other analysts and specialists were focused on Homeland Security and the conspiracy; sorting out fact from fiction. They were monitoring the identification of the men killed in Pierre, the Pierre police officers and movement of Homeland Security and TSA employees.

"Whoo-hoo, I'm in!" shouted Blake jumping up. He tipped over the hula dancing penguin on his desk. He quickly started copying the files and then did his own hula dance.

His manager entered Blake's office with a zip drive in his hand.
"I heard the good news, we just got the names of some of the men killed in Pierre, compare these to their lists – go ahead and check everyone who is involved in the investigation against their database. Good work Blake."

$$* \qquad * \qquad * \qquad *$$

In the Deputy Directors Executive Briefing room the FBI leaders met to review and update the team on the conspiracy in Pierre.

On the video monitor was a photo of Joe Smith, the man Jerry killed in his plane – the man who started the whole mess.

"Ladies and Gentlemen, on the monitor you see the nexus of this conspiracy. Due to the hard work of the Pierre police, the South Dakota crime lab, our analysts and agents… and a little luck, we have the connection between this attempted terrorist attack and Homeland Security. The surprising outcome is the real root of this conspiracy," the Deputy Director explained.

Next on the screen were the photo IDs and names of the 8 Homeland Security subcontractors.

"These men," the Director continued, "died in a failed operation to kidnap Jerry Sherwood's family and ensure his cooperation. We have a direct connection from these men, their pay, the vehicles and even their equipment -- to Homeland Security."

"The twist is these men, who were following orders, were murdered in a sloppy attempt to cover their tracks by a third party with a remote controlled explosive device in the truck and magnesium used as an accelerant," The Director said dramatically.

"Each truck had audio and video cameras inside them and they were transmitting to an unknown remote location – we did not overlook the fact that none of these soldiers fired at our officers," added the Director.

The next slide on the screens showed a moving collage of all the men's photos rotating around a box with a big question mark.

"The big break just came, one of our best Computer Security Specialists was able to access the genealogy database of the Church of Latter Day Saints. When we matched our list of victims and conspiracy suspects all the puzzle pieces fell into place. All the conspirators and suspects are members of the Mormon Church with significant genealogical history going back generations," he proudly announced.

The next screen was a diagram of the states of the United States. A star was located at Pierre, South Dakota and there were four red lines.

"Next, I am grateful we were able to locate and intercept three of the four attack sites," He said while pointing to the screen.

"We allowed the operations in Ohio, Wisconsin and California to occur and we let them tell their superiors they were successful before intercepting them."

"The one operation near Rochester, Minnesota was intercepted in the same manner by the team of Jerry Sherwood and Galen Anderson, Chief of the Pierre police department. We have a field agent with them now as they travel towards Salt Lake City."

The Deputy Director paused and looked around the briefing room and slowly and quietly said, "Our job is not yet done, we still believe there is something bigger than the Church of Latter day Saints. We need more focused research and investigation into the Mormon Church and its connection Homeland Security and this conspiracy. We need to find the source of the bacteria and the motive." In a whisper he added, "Of course this is very secret and critical."

Chapter 42
Salt Lake City, Utah

W hat a beautiful morning; Madam Leader was beaming, big smile, a jump in her step, her shoulders back; she was wallowing in her success. She giggled when she passed the security checkpoint. One of the guards heard her and asked, "Excuse me, Madam Leader?"

"Mind your own business, Officer." She said curtly. "And tighten your tie and stand up straight – where is your Mormon pride? This is a great day for our church," she lectured him as she brushed by.

When she arrived at the Operations Room, she announced, "Give me an overnight briefing in two minutes." The associates all jerked alert at her voice and started getting their materials together.

Madam Leader's daughter, Mary Rose rolled her eyes— her mother always blustered too much. She also knew enough to stay out of her way when she was in this mood.

"Operation Mothers Milk. What is the status?" Madam leader asked. The associates responded around the table;

"All packages delivered."
"No more agents lost."
"Cover up going well."
"We are on target for budget and timeline."
"Our plants are on goal."

"This is great, but are there no new opportunities for leveraged manipulation?" she asked. Leveraged manipulation was idiomatic for blackmail and extortion.

"Keep up the good work, keep to the plan and be ready for the chaos." She made eye contact with each of them and said, "Don't screw this up, let's stay together on this and communicate with each other."

She excused them and went back to her office. Mary Rose poked her head in and reported, trying to please, "I am still looking for more information on the legislators but it is slow going; I have my team doing more research on Jerry Sherwood and his family."

"Don't worry about Jerry, find his wife and family," her mother replied with a tone of annoyance.

"Leave me while I do some work." She waved her hand and looked away.

She pulled out her little black book, called a number on the east coast and took a deep breath.

"Hello Jimmy," she said with sarcastic lilt. "It's so nice to talk with you again,"

"What do you want?" Jimmy hissed. "What? No, 'Hey, how ya doing,' or 'So good to hear from you?'" she said in that sarcastic smarmy voice.

"WHAT do you want?" he asked again.
"I'm just checking in with you, seeing how your family is doing. How is your wife? Your daughter in school?" she asked with fake sincerity.

143

"I need to know what your agency knows about our little adventure," she asked.

"We know you were successful, and you screwed up the cover up." he said with some satisfaction. He wanted her to think she had been successful.

"What are your agency's next steps?" she followed up.

"We are looking at the evidence in Pierre, we are also looking for Jerry Sherwood and Galen Anderson," Jimmy said, trying to sound genuine and truthful.

After a tiny pause she said, "What else do you know?"

"I know you and I have a relationship that is a 'No win' relationship." Then he added, "…and, it will soon end. Working with you is worse than the effects of my little problems."

"OK, if that's the way you want it, I have a wonderful video file and supporting documents ready to send anonymously to your boss. I just want to help you get what you want," she said calling his bluff.

He needed to let her think her plan was succeeding so he said, "Well, no, that can wait. How much longer will you be harassing me?" "What are your plans?" he asked. "What do I know that you can use?" he pleaded.

"Mmmm, Jimmy Dear, you are much less attractive when you are desperate," she said trying to be patronizing. "You will be done when I say you are done." This time she said it with cold, calculated menace.

"I've killed dozens of men, women and children. Killing you would be so easy," she said in a whisper.

The call was over – all he heard was a dial tone.
Jimmy looked up to the Deputy Director who was listening in.

"Wow, she's a bitch, a spooky, crazy bitch," he said with raised eyebrows.

"You're sure this fake information will never get out?" Jimmy said hopefully.

"This information was just for her, and only her. We had to make it believable and serious, but it's all fixable," he reassured him. "You done good."

Chapter 43
45 Miles South West of Sioux Falls, South Dakota

"How are you doing back there?" Jerry turned to Galen in the back seat and asked. "Are you hit? Are you OK?" he insisted.

Galen was wide eyed in the back seat as he put his finger through the bullet hole in the floor and then he put his finger through the hole in the roof.

"Man, what a day I am having, this is either the luckiest or the most unlucky day I have ever had," Galen announced.

FBI Agent Elliot Ray examined the hole in the roof from the front seat

"Any damage to the plane, you know, other than the hole?" They inspected what they could see and reach and found no apparent additional damage.

The eastern sky was starting to glow. The sky over head was a deep dark blue and gradually blended to violet and then to orange. They were gradually climbing to between 1,000 and 2,000 feet above the ground. The trip west would take them over rising terrain all the way through the Rocky Mountains to Salt Lake City, Utah.

"Who was that shooting at us?" Jerry asked naively.

"Likely Homeland Security, you and Galen know too much," Elliot warned without taking his eyes off the aviation sectional map. "We must take extra precautions to avoid detection, one of our strongest weapons will be surprise."

"We will need fuel in less than two hours, I found a little airport that will allow us to get fuel without detection. Medicine Bow, Wyoming." Jerry said.

"Is it on the way? Let's go there." Galen said with a huge yawn. "I am starting to fade guys, I should get some sleep."

Riding in small planes puts a lot of people to sleep. The droning engine, the rocking motion and the high altitude lack of oxygen all combine to rock people to sleep. Galen had been up for almost 24 hours straight – he needed sleep.

In the quiet of a dark night with the engine and propeller roar, a person's mind wanders.

Elliot had periodic flashbacks from Iraq – when he saw the rifle flashes and then the bang as the slug went through the plane. He had all the same feelings of being right in the middle of an attack as he was flying his helicopter picking up soldiers under attack. The bullets ricocheted off the armor of the helicopter and tore through the fuselage where there was no armor.

He had to fight the fear and worked hard to remain in the present and not get distracted. The fact that they were shot at was not a good sign, they would be continuously pursued and in constant danger.

Would Homeland Security send fighter jets after them? How about the Warthog assault plane or any of the assault helicopters, even the unmanned aerial vehicle Predator could carry rockets or missiles. They would be sitting ducks if attacked. Their only defense would be stealth and surprise.

"How did they find us so quickly? How are they tracking us?" Elliot asked rhetorically.

Jerry said, "We used no GPS, all cell phones are off…" He then reached into his coat pocket and remembered the phone he picked up from one of the guys who sabotaged the milk plant. He pulled it out of his pocket and opened it up – he had not turned it off. He looked at Elliot with an embarrassed and frightened look.

Elliot grabbed the phone and said, "Wait, this could be very useful, think about this, first it is full of great phone numbers—evidence. It could be a direct line to the person who is pulling the strings." He turned it off, smiled and said, "I have a good feeling about this."

Jerry was embarrassed; he may have exposed his friends to more risk. He really was not suited for this mission. He was not feeling confident at all. They are being chased because he killed Joe Smith.

Elliot kept the conversation light to keep Jerry focused on flying and navigating the plane. They talked about planes and pilots and training and engines and instruments. It was a good thing that Galen was asleep because listening to two aviation nuts talk about planes can drive a non aviation person crazy.

Sunrise turned into another warm morning. Long shadows over the rolling fields changed into a penetrating sunlight pouring energy into the soil for the seeds and young plants.

"How did you get this plane again?" Elliot asked.

Jerry told the story of how one of the conspirators was his acquaintance Bob, he used to be a buddy but soon would be referred only as 'that co –conspirator'.

A Flying Adventure

Elliot and Jerry watched the land change beneath them. They were low enough to see details on the ground as the flat green fields transitioned to rougher small hills and dirt and rock between green prairie grasses. As they got closer to Medicine Bow, Wyoming they gradually climbed. The Tea, South Dakota airport elevation was 1515 feet and their destination airport, Medicine Bow airport elevation was 6646 feet above sea level.

Even at 2000 feet above the ground they could see a long way in the distance—small hills in the foreground and larger hills, then small mountains and behind them large snow capped mountain peaks.

Elliot looked back at Galen sleeping in the backseat, slumped over the extra gear in duffle bags. He watched Jerry scan the horizon and monitor the engine instruments. The fuel gauge indicated they were getting low on fuel – one wing tank was empty and the other was about 1/3 full.

"How are you doing, Jerry?" he asked.

"I am good, but I am worried about my wife and kids," he replied, adjusting his lucky cap.

"They'll be fine; they know how to stay out of sight. This will be over in a day or so I expect," Elliot said. "I was really asking about you, Jerry. Even experienced agents have to adjust after their first fatal weapons use. We need you to be at peak performance."

"I think I'm OK, I just need to focus on flying and I will be fine." Jerry said while looking away from Elliot.

They flew in silence for about 30 minutes.

"How are we doing on fuel?" Elliot asked pointing at the fuel gauges.

"We have been delayed by a pretty strong head wind, I slowed down to conserve fuel, by my calculations we will have plenty of fuel to reach Medicine Bow," Jerry said confidently.

"Elliot, why can't the FBI fix all the mis-information about us? Everybody who watches the news thinks we are fugitives and they are reporting I have a dirty bomb. Will we ever be able to clear our names?" Jerry asked furtively.

Elliot's mind was racing considering all the alternatives and trying to make a plan that would give the greatest chance for success. He was considering how much to tell Jerry. He only needed to know what was necessary for the task at hand.

"Jerry, your name will be cleared, I am working on a plan, wait until you see what I brought!" he exclaimed while pointing over his shoulder.

"But we are three, and the FBI is big, well trained, with tools and resources. Just get some search warrants and go into their headquarters and get the evidence," Jerry suggested.

"Before they kidnapped my parents I learned they had plenty of evidence, but the FBI wants to get those at the root of the conspiracy." Elliot explained further.

"Then if we go after the Mormon Church, won't we be screwing up the plan?" Jerry asked.

"I'll tell you everything I know and my plan when we land, so I can tell Galen at the same time."

"OK, we're close, about 30 miles out. We should have checked the Airport Facility Guide earlier, Elliot, do me a favor, read what it says about Medicine Bow," Jerry asked as he was going through the pre-landing checklist.

"Medicine Bow, Wyoming, it says here, 'Runway may have gopher holes, rough dirt runway with a one foot ditch." Elliot read with disbelief. "We can't land there!"

"That's exactly why we are landing there, besides we need to get fuel and take a break."

Jerry flew over the runway at about 500 feet to check it out. He noticed tire tracks that turned about 1/3 of the way down the runway. There were no taxi ways, planes had to back taxi on the runway to take off. The lack of tire tracks on one end indicated the runway was extra rough there. "We need to plan on touch down so we too avoid those ruts," Jerry remarked.

Elliot knew to keep quiet during landing to reduce distractions for the pilot. Jerry went through his landing checklist, boost, fuel pump, carb heat (to prevent carb ice), gas (switch to the tank with the most fuel in it) mixture to rich and finally prop to landing configuration.

He put in flaps, reduced power and watched the airspeed to prevent it from getting to slow. On final Jerry and Elliot could see the runway was not at all level—it fell off to the left then the right and there was a small hill in the middle. As they got closer they saw a very rough runway.

Jerry held the plane off as long as possible so the plane was as slow as possible. The wheels touched down – they were in and out of ruts, then a big hole and the hump in the middle of the runway, they were airborne for a bit then back on the ground. Then a large crash, one of the main wheels went in and out of a gopher hole in a second and the wheel pant flew off and shattered into about 20 pieces. Pieces of the fiberglass wheel cover spread out over the dirt runway, plumes of dust were kicked up by the wheels and wake turbulence.

The plane kicked to the side of the big gopher hole, Jerry instantly countered to the right. Galen was jostled awake, "What the…," he yelled.

Elliot warned, "Stay right if you can." Jerry kept the nose wheel off the ground by pulling back on the yoke and pushed the right rudder pedal. When the plane slowed a bit more he started gentle braking.

They taxied to the only building on the airport. There was a fuel tank and an old style gas pump. They pulled up to the pump and shut down the engine.

"That's a hell of a runway, this must be Medicine Bow," Galen complained while stretching after climbing out of the plane.

"Actually a very good landing – we don't need that wheel pant anyway!" Elliot said with a laugh.

"There is an old saying in racing cars – 'Drive it like you ain't got a dime in it' I don't really care about the wheel pant—it ain't my plane!" Jerry said with a snicker.

On the gas pump was a sign that directed them to call a number and the airport manager would be out to pump the gas. Elliot called on his cell phone so they would need to wait.

Galen stretched his legs, Jerry was on his back looking at the bullet hole in the belly of the plane and looking for other damage.

Elliot grabbed his duffle bags and started digging. He pulled out protein bars and Gatorade for everyone. Galen and

Jerry stood by the plane and the three of them were quiet as they ate and drank.

Chapter 44
Medicine Bow Airport, Wyoming

"Elliot, you talked in the air about a plan, what is the plan?" Jerry said. Pilots want a plan, he has told his friends many times 'Plan your work and work your plan.'

"As you know I worked in Salt Lake City at the FBI field office for two years. The Church of Latter Day Saints was a target of investigation but we always ran into road blocks or just thin air." He took a deep drink and continued. "The church itself is squeaky clean and until now we had no concrete connection to any domestic terrorism."

"In the local field office we believed the headquarters for a mysterious branch of the church was inside a small building that had a long distance sales call center as a cover."

"My plan is to get in, use my homemade surveillance equipment, gather evidence and then get a confession on tape."

"Wait a minute, if we break in, won't that evidence be thrown out—no conviction?" Jerry asked looking at both Galen and Elliot.

Then Galen interrupted, "We might not get the conviction but our names will be cleared."

"But can't we get both our names cleared and a conviction – there is murder here, conspiracy, attempted terrorism?" Jerry asked.

After a pause Elliot said, "We need more information, Galen, you should call the Pierre police and get an update, I can call a trusted friend in the FBI and at least find out what they know. I know the phones will probably be monitored but it's worth the risk."

"At noon I need to call my wife. I wonder when the fuel guy will be here?" Jerry said as he looked down the road into the very small town.

Galen turned his cell phone on and called the Pierre police department. The dispatcher answered, "Chief Anderson! Is that really you?"

"Yes, I am OK, but I need information—tell me the most recent information," he asked, all business.

"Homeland Security locked us up until the FBI came to our rescue. Bob is still missing. The trucks and men who were blown up and burned were contractors for Homeland Security – all former military men. The two who kidnapped Jerry and his wife were Homeland Security. There is a ton of information connecting this conspiracy with Homeland Security but nothing concrete to the Mormon Church. We haven't heard anything about the bacteria in milk plants. Jerry's shirt had DNA from the guy who kidnapped him—another former military," she whispered.

"Homeland Security, in our station? And the staff was jailed?" Galen asked unbelieving.

"Yea, the Homeland Security Commander was a real jerk but he came around and we are working together OK." the dispatcher said with a shrug and a smirk.

"OK, do what the FBI commander asks, don't tell anyone I called, follow your procedures." Galen hung up the phone. He was reaching to turn it off when he received a call, it was Her. He looked around to make sure he could not be over heard and walked away from the plane.

"Oh Gay-len," she said in a sarcastic sing - song. "Galen how is my favorite police chief? Are you having fun on your adventure?"

"What do you want?" he asked annoyed.

"I asked you nicely to watch Jerry, what have you to report," she said in a curt manner.

"Jerry thinks we can go to Salt Lake City and just ask people on the street for the person responsible for the misinformation," Galen bluffed. "He's harmless, but I am useless to you if your media misinformation campaign still includes me," Galen urged.

"I can be more use to everyone if I am cleared immediately." He was trying to manipulate the champion manipulator. "Oh, forget it, screw you, I'm done."

"Wait, wait…..wait a second Galen, just slow down a bit. I'll take care of you; your secret is safe with me. I'll work on clearing your name," she conceded.

"What's your status?"

"We are grounded—some kind of mechanical problem with the wheel of the plane, Jerry is working on it. We'll be here for maybe a day—need to get parts." This time Galen hung up on her and turned his phone off.

*　　　*　　　*　　　*

Elliot said he was calling his friend in the FBI for information but he was calling the Deputy Director.

"Elliot! Am I glad to hear from you. We have more information. The target is a woman called Madam Leader – a secret group of women who are actually above the men in the organization of the Church of Later Day Saints. This woman is treacherous and resourceful. You are the best person for this mission."

"We are in Medicine Bow, Wyoming, we have some gear but we need more," Elliot said.

"We need to move quickly, they do not know that we are on to them, we think they will run and hide if we wait." The Deputy Director continued, "You have support from the highest level of the FBI. We have some questions about the Salt Lake City Field office loyalty – if you contact them be careful. We will be monitoring the staff there but we do not have additional resources on the ground yet so you are on your own. We are not sure how long we can hold off the information from them.

We intercepted all the bacteria, we are tracking the perpetrators but when the tainted milk does not flow and make people sick, they will know they have been exposed," the Deputy Director added seriously.

"I have a plan. I can get in, intercept their internal audio and video and send it to you." Elliot offered.

The Deputy Director asked, "And then what?"
"Watch the feed and have your best agents ready to bust in," Elliot requested.

"We'll have the search warrant by the time you get there. How are the other guys doing?" the concerned Deputy Director asked.

"They're OK, it could be worse and it could be better. I can make it work." Elliot added quietly. "I haven't seen anything suspicious in Galen yet and I am worried about Jerry."

"Keep your eyes open, we'll be monitoring your progress," the Deputy Director ended the call.

*　　*　　*　　*

While Galen and Elliot were on the phone, the airport manager arrived and began fueling the plane. The airport manager was an older man who had not used a razor in years. He arrived in a 40 year old pickup with an engine running on five of six cylinders. Jerry watched him and he tried to hide his face just in case the airport manager had seen the television reports.

Jerry wasn't interested in small talk and the airport manager seemed to ignore the guys.

Finally Jerry said nervously, "We are going hunting." The airport manager shrugged his shoulders, put the hose away and collected the cash and left in his beat up pickup.

The plane was full of fuel, inspected and ready to roll. Jerry watched the time – he needed to call his wife at noon. Galen and Elliot were making preparations to leave, looking over at Jerry. Jerry pointed to his watch.

Finally, noon, Jerry turned on his phone and called Lynn. No answer. "Oh no," he whispered.

Elliot yelled over to Jerry, "You've got about 25 seconds."
He dialed again, the phone rang and Lynn answered, "Jerry?"

"Yea, honey it's me. We have 25 seconds—first I need to say I love you and the kids. Is everything OK?"

"I love you too and I miss you, we are good, safe, no problems," Lynn answers quickly.

"Lynn, I have one word, Oshkosh. I gotta go. Fly safe." The call was over.

Chapter 45
Medicine Bow Wyoming

J erry turned off his phone and sprinted to the plane, "OK guys, let's go!"

He quickly strapped in, went over the preflight checklist and warmed up the engine while back taxiing on the rough runway. Elliot and Galen were stowing all the gear to make sure the luggage was stored securely.

On a dirt runway there is always a chance the vortices from the prop could stir up rocks or stones and then hit the prop. To prevent damage the pilot must keep moving and keep the engine speed down until ready to take off.

They taxied very slowly over the rough ground. Jerry saw where other pilots turned around—there was still 5,000 feet of runway. He pushed the throttle to full power and started the rough take off roll. He pulled the yoke back slightly to lighten the pressure on the front wheel. They were at a higher elevation, less air molecules to push against so it takes much longer to get off the ground.

As they gain speed, they began to float over the bumps and finally they became airborne, barely.

They built speed slowly in a nearly flat climb angle and when they were high enough gently turned west through a pass. The cabin was quiet; the men knew this was a risky endeavor.

Next stop was Salt Lake City Municipal Airport, a small non-towered airport just inside the city limits they could get to without contacting the tower for the main airport in Salt Lake City.

Elliot said, "We need some more equipment, I have a good friend who works for a large hunting store, he will deliver the gear and a vehicle for us to use."

Jerry announced, "We've got some big mountains in front of us, the scenery will be tremendous but I will need your help."

They settled in for the next leg of the trip.

Chapter 45
The Circle K Motel, Broken Bow, Nebraska

What did Jerry mean by Oshkosh? She figured either he or she was being monitored and they could triangulate to locate them both.

They went to Airventure, the largest flyin and aviation convention in the world, at Oshkosh just about every year. They camp on the field and see thousands of planes and just about anything aviation related. What did he mean?

When they fly they always stop at the Springfield, Minnesota airport, a cool - old style airport in a small friendly town.

She could fly to Oshkosh but it was a towered airport that could be watched by TSA – he must mean Springfield. There was a motel within walking distance, hangar space to rent and fuel on the field.

"Come on kids, time to go, another little trip, get your bags," she said to the kids. They were ready to go – it was boring there. "Does the next motel have a pool?" "Let's go to a place with a pool" they asked.

"We'll see," was all Lynn said.

Chapter 46
FBI Headquarters

The Deputy Director and the Project Hotel Sierra Team moved large white boards on wheels into the largest available conference room. They put photos, names and background information on an affinity diagram with lines drawn between the murdered people. The lines all led back to six different Director level positions in Homeland Security.

They also identified which people on the white board who were listed in the Mormon Church Genealogy database --all of whom had direct lineage to the original pioneers who traveled to Utah to establish the territories.

The FBI Deputy Director took a position in front of the white boards cleared his throat loudly and said, "Three of the Directors are connected but the other three must have some other connection – we need more information on them."

"We have been monitoring a shadowy group of people with Mormon funding and support. This woman is the leader and we have irrefutable evidence that she is blackmailing individuals to manipulate them to do what she wants."

"Are we confident that the conspiracy is only at the Director level?" asked the manager.

"We do not believe the front line agents are involved but we are not confident the corruption does not extend up the chain of command," the Hotel Sierra manager reported.

The Director continued, "I would like to reach out to Homeland Security and offer to help, but how high do we need to go and how do we know who can be trusted?"

"Can we get their front line agents interested in the conspiracy and have them do the inside work?" said the manager.

"Would the Justice Department have the resources and availability to dig?"

"I want everything we can find on this woman and then I want all of you to focus on these three Homeland Security Directors, and anyone else who has any kind of relationship, even coincidental, with this woman," he said tapping his hand on a grainy photo on the white board.

"We are running out of time—right now they think they have gotten away with this conspiracy but soon they will realize we are on to them and then they will disappear into the woodwork like roaches when lights are turned on."

"Pierre, South Dakota is under control thanks to our field agents there, we believe the Homeland Security and TSA field agents are not involved—they are doing what they are told but they could be used against the conspirators."

"We do not know yet how high they have their blackmailing interests, so be careful," The Deputy Director cautioned.

"We have a search warrant for her headquarters in Salt Lake City and we have a small undercover team working on it. We also suspect there may be an FBI agent under her control so trust, but verify everything, from everyone."

With his final comments, he nodded his head and everyone in the room rushed out to continue their research.

The Deputy Director followed the Project Hotel Sierra manager back to her office. He closed the door and sat down with a frown on his face.

"Prepare for a transmission from our agent and get a team on the ground in Salt Lake ready to roll – let's not tell the Salt Lake Office – I think there is a leak there – someone who has been in Salt Lake too long. The local law enforcement are also unreliable."

"I want you to lead this mission – I have been away from tactical operations for too long, we need someone who can lead objectively and ruthlessly, I am too close. I think you are the best person for this operation." He said solemnly.

The manager swallowed loudly and then smiled. She recognized a great opportunity.

Chapter 47
Salt Lake City, Utah

Madam Leader went to church with her husband and her daughter. She played the role of the subservient wife in public. She sat with her family and other Leadership Council members in the front row.

She smiled and shook hands and hugged her friends. Her daughter, Mary Rose, sat in the next row with her husband. Madam Leader was conflicted – she wanted her daughter to progress through the organization normally but she would be in the way. She asked again about the prospects of a granddaughter. Madam Leader must treat her own daughter like all of her rivals – without mercy.

Very few people knew she was at the top of the Leadership Council – only the top apostles – the top 6 men in the church knew her true position in the church.

She and the Leadership Council did the dirty work for the church. They handled the politics, they coordinated the influence, they brokered the favors, and kept the church separated from the dirty business of politics.

The Leadership Council had been organized by the women of the church almost 150 years ago. The men were distracted with religion and business but no one was paying attention to politics, so the women stepped forward. As in many cultures, the women were the best at adapting to their situation – in this situation the women organized and worked together to solve the problem.

Women were groomed for leadership through their work in the church and their skills in manipulation and subterfuge. They competed with each other for the top job—survival of the sleaziest.

Madam Leader also had something on each of the top apostles. She watched them and waited until they did something human, something she can twist to maintain her position of power. Even when the apostles were clean, she would manipulate them into compromising positions.

She had the ability to compartmentalize and rationalize her activities. She said she did it all for the church – to protect the church, to allow the church to grow.

She didn't do it for money – she had everything she needed even though she earned less than her husband. She didn't do it for fame or attention; she gladly played the public role of a typical Mormon wife.

She loved the power, she loved that she could order her people around, she was proud of the fact that she had at least 100 men under her influence. These men were powerful, rich, influential and fallible. She loved to see these powerful men whimper, and cower to her demands. She got physically aroused when she made her demand calls to her men. In her mind she thought she was taking care of them, protecting them.

If scientists measured her endorphins and adrenaline when she was working her men, the readings would be at the top of the chart. Now she was addicted to the rush, she needed the excitement, she craved the power. The need was to be her strength and her weakness.

Chapter 48
Broken Bow Airport, Broken Bow Nebraska

L ynn got a ride back to the airport, the attendant was extra helpful moving the plane out of the hangar and filling it with fuel. Women are underrepresented in aviation and she <u>was</u> very cute and confident – guys did things for her all the time.

She looked for a sectional map of the Twin Cities area and folded it so she could access it easily. She made a flight plan and had a compass heading and had the navigational aids lined up for the trip. It should take about 3 hours to fly the route.

While she loaded the plane, she scanned the airport for strangers. The Broken Bow airport is small and remote, no people, no traffic, so she was confident she was safe.

She paid the attendant cash and a little tip and got in the plane. The kids were buckled in and quieter than normal.
"OK kids; are you ready for another adventure? This is kind of fun traveling together," she said hopefully.

"It would be more fun if they had a pool." "Does the next place have a pool, Mom?" they asked while squirming in their seats. Lynn just smiled and rolled her eyes.

Lynn warmed up the engine, checked the instruments and carefully taxied out to the runway end for take off.

She looked around and noticed an unmarked helicopter flying low across the field. She was monitoring the local communication frequency for the airport and there were no calls so she called out, "Broken Bow traffic, this is Piper 231 Charlie Alfa, ready for take off on runway zero four, helicopter in the area what are you intentions?"

There was no answer and she was getting concerned. The helicopter landed in the middle of the runway and stayed there with its engine running – rotor spinning. Lynn saw the paved runway was not wide enough to get around but she felt a strong need to get away. For her there was no choice of fight or flight—she needed to get out of there.

She had seen airports with parallel turf runways next to the paved runway. The area to the left of the paved runway was not turf – it was more weeds and crabgrass but it looked smooth enough. She applied full power, gradually went off the pavement and put in ½ flaps for a short field take off. The take off run was longer than on pavement—the plants and soft soil slowed her down. She was not airborne by the time they passed the helicopter. The helicopter had applied full power before the plane passed by creating a strong wind from the helicopter rotor blades. The plane veered to the left, about the same time lifted off. She counteracted the turbulence and made a shallow left hand turn; she pulled the flaps off gently and continued her full power climb on a North East heading.

The helicopter was trying to chase them but even a slow Piper is faster than the turbine powered, fully loaded helicopter.

She continued the climb until she was 3,000 feet about the ground.

"That was interesting, huh kids?" She said to her kids. They were trying to be brave but they were scared and pretty quiet.

Lynn flew as fast as she could but she worried every second who would be chasing her. Would they try to shoot her down? Should she land and hide out?   Who are the good guys here?   What about her children!

Springfield is about 250 miles away, Jerry would say, 'Plan your work, and work your plan.' She had her eyes open for other traffic more than on a normal flight.

"Hey kids, I need your help, look for other planes." She was worried but tried to keep a positive outlook.

Chapter 49
Western Wyoming

The terrain was much rougher, fewer landing areas, more and larger mountains. Jerry kept I 80 in view as he snaked through the passes. A highway makes a fair emergency landing area. The flight has been smooth except around the downwind side of mountains.

Jerry slowed the plane a bit. As he scanned the horizon he was momentarily distracted by the beautiful scenery. Fluffy clouds at about 9,000 feet. They were flying at 8,000 feet mean sea level taking them in and out of turbulence,

"How are you guys doing?" Jerry asked.

Galen was busy watching the terrain, the mountains, the valleys and rivers. "This is wonderful; I've lived my whole life on the South Dakota prairie. This view is awesome!"

"I'm gonna need some clean clothes, a shave and shower and some real food when we get to Salt Lake City," he added.

Elliot spoke up, "I got you covered, my buddy is delivering the goods – but we will have to eat on the way."

"I gotta start eating better food," Galen admitted

The plane was running great, they had a plan, and were hopeful. Doing something was better than doing nothing.

They saw clear creeks and muddy rivers winding through the hills and valleys. There were green plateaus and rocky mountains under them.   They flew around snow tipped peaks. Browns and grays spotted with deep evergreens covered the ground under the plane.   This flight would be a picturesque trip if it were not such a dangerous and critical event.

.

Chapter 50
FBI Headquarters Washington, DC

The analysts and researchers had been looking for hours for information on the woman known as Madam Leader. In a darkened meeting room a screen displayed photos, the team of analysts took turns sharing what they had learned about each of the conspirators and suspects.

"Her name is Vera Smith, age 56, born in a small town 50 miles south of Salt Lake City. She completed the 10th grade, no college, no additional training other than religion training at the church," one of the analysts reported to the manager.

"She has no credit cards, no subscriptions, no email addresses, she has a drivers license, but no tickets, no criminal history, minimal investments, no real estate or property," reported another analyst.

"This is juicy; she has 2 children, her son was killed in the kidnapping attempt of Jerry Sherwood and her daughter works for, well, she is paid through, the same long distance phone sales company," a third analyst reported.

"The company is a shell for the Mormon Church, the sign on the door and the website says Smith and Associates but that's all that is genuine. We have some information but have not gotten all the way into their systems. They have an odd - enigmatic information security system; we're still working on that"

"It's funny we can get into any bank account and email but have not yet gotten into their computers."

"She has one hobby, audio video systems; she's spent $40,000 on her home office system."

The Deputy Director interjected, "Guys, I invited one of our Profilers to sit in and help, Agent Derek Petersen." The Deputy Director motioned with his arm for Derek to stand. "You've read the reports, what do you think?"

Derek paused, scanned the screen and looked at the Agents and Analysts around the table and said, "She is a borderline psychopath with narcissistic features and a personality disorder. She is not motivated by money or recognition; she uses her religion to mask her rage and frustration. This is a very dangerous person who has absolutely no remorse and can act brutally without hesitation."

"She will never commit suicide – she will always think she has the upper hand but if cornered she will sacrifice anything, including family to save herself or reach her goal."

"She manages with fear and intimidation which makes her subordinates fiercely loyal until backed into a corner when they will fold like a cheap lawn chair."

With that last sentence the profiler paused, looked around the room and sat down.

"Thanks a lot guys, this is all great information that we can share with our field agents. We have a team set to infiltrate the organization to gather information, the audio and video will be sent using their satellite communication system, so be ready," the Deputy Director's tone was urgent.

"We still need information about who else she is black mailing. We need to trace this back to all those involved. We need to do this now while they still have their guard down. I've

174

decided to bring in another group to assist; they come directly from the President and will report to me. I will share the information with your team. This project is your top priority."

"Our agents are going in today, let's get this right!"

Chapter 51
30 miles east of Salt Lake City, Utah

Jerry, Galen and Elliot were getting close and began preparations for landing. Elliot sent a text message to his friend confirming their imminent arrival. His friend had the additional gear and a vehicle for them to use. Elliot also sent a message to the Deputy Director informing him of their progress, and that he was looking for any more information about the target and the FBI investigation.

Jerry monitored the Air Traffic Control Tower frequency at the Salt Lake City International Airport. He had the sectional on his lap and was checking the borders of the class B airspace. Class B airspace is area around the larger airports where entry permission from the tower is required and this trio wanted to avoid attention.

Their destination was a smaller airport with a smaller runway where they will be little or no activity. The Salt Lake City Municipal Airport, about 20 miles south of the International airport, will be a good compromise between convenience and security. They would be able to minimize their exposure to Transportation Security Administration.

Galen was in the back seat taking another nap. Before he nodded off, he had been digging through Elliot's duffle bags, smiling as he went through the equipment and tools. He seemed satisfied because he fell asleep holding his weapon with a silencer and a large knife in its sheath.

Jerry turned south and approached the airport through a pass south of the class B airspace. All morning he had been flying around the largest peaks and working to stay on course using the navigation aids, a map and compass and keeping the GPS off. He had been so busy he has not thought about food; Lynn had to remind him to stay hydrated because he would often forget. Jerry reached for his bottle of water and finished it wondering how Lynn was doing.

"What if Lynn is in trouble again, I should be with her and taking care of my family and I'm here," Jerry asked after a very long period of silence.

Elliot looked at Jerry, then at Galen, asleep in the back seat and then looked straight ahead. After another long pause he said, "Jerry, you are thinking you should be with your wife, you are not confident you can contribute; the closer we get the more you are having second thoughts about this project."

Jerry looked at Elliot; he did not need to say a word. Elliot read in Jerry's face that his analysis was correct.

Elliot could tell Jerry needed some hope and a bit of a distraction, "Here's my secret weapon."

Elliot pulled out an electronic gadget that was duct taped together. He hooked it into the intercom system. He turned on the switch and rows of lights began blinking. "It's a radio scanner on steroids!" Elliot proudly announced.

"With this we can listen, not just police, but the encrypted digital signals of Homeland Security, the FBI and any security force using communication radios." Elliot said with a confident smile.

"That is cool; let's get it fired up because we are about 15 minutes from touch down," Jerry cautioned.

"We needed to wait until we had cleared that ridge – now we have a clear signal from the entire valley," Elliot announced.

Jerry dialed in the common traffic frequency for the Salt Lake City Municipal Airport and announced their location and intention to land.

Elliot nudged Galen in the back seat and said, "We're close, wake up and get ready!" Galen groaned and pulled himself together – he was alert in seconds.

"Salt Lake Muni traffic, this is Cessna Niner, Niner, Delta Juliet, 10 miles south, inbound for runway three four," Jerry announced over the airport frequency. Pilots at non towered airports communicate on the common traffic frequency giving their identification, their location and intention. The group had been traveling between small airports for two days, now they are about to land at a busier airport in the middle of a major metropolitan city. Jerry monitored the airport frequency and Elliot listened to the police and other law enforcement radio chatter.

Jerry needed to blend in with a small training plane and a pair of military helicopters. He entered the pattern on the upwind leg and checked out the airport grounds – he was looking for black SUV's with tinted windows.

Along the way he reduced speed and got the plane ready for landing with flaps, and engine adjustments. He turned base, then final and reduced power for touchdown. He reminded himself to keep flying the plane until the engine was shut down. The main wheels touched then a few seconds later the nose wheel and some gentle braking and an easy turn off the runway to the taxiway.

Arriving safely at the destination always gave Jerry a strong sense of accomplishment. Seeing the airport before him caused Jerry to smile. Flying is fun – it's a rush -- and a blast. He didn't tell Elliot or Galen this was his first flight through mountains. The trip had gone perfectly; the weather was ideal, their navigation was right on, the landing was flawless. If he wasn't in so much trouble he would have thought he was having a great day.

Chapter 52
Salt Lake City, Utah

"There's his truck, taxi over there and be ready to move," Elliot commanded. He just heard some coded communication on a digital encrypted frequency through his scanner that made him very anxious.

"I think they are coming so let's motivate," He warned his comrades.

Jerry shut down the engine over a tie down spot and the beige pick up owned by Elliot's friend pulled up to the plane.

Elliot jumped out and shouted, "Hi John, thanks for getting this together, unfortunately we gotta run. I just picked up a communication that they are on their way."

John was a young bearded mountain man with a hearty laugh and a big smile. "I understand. Is some lady's husband after you?" he said as he pulled his personal gear out of the truck.

As the crew was getting in the truck, John said, "I'll take care of the plane. I got a buddy who can give me a ride."

Galen found the clean change of clothes and changed his pants and shirt right there. He was still wearing the Pierre Police Department uniform and smelled like a football team locker room. Jerry looked in the bags for food; he was hungry and thirsty again.

"I'll need to switch the truck with another vehicle later," John yelled as they drove off.

Elliot sat in the drivers' seat, Jerry was in the middle and Galen was in the shotgun seat, with an actual shotgun in his lap.

They heard screeching tires before they saw the pair of black SUV's. Elliot knew they were coming so he accelerated solidly but smoothly between hangars and out the main gate while the Homeland Security trucks parked in front and behind the plane. They exited their trucks with guns drawn. They yelled at the plane but it was empty.

John walked away and traveled between the hangars until he got to the airport pilot's lounge, grabbed a magazine and sat down. One Homeland Security team entered the lounge which was also the office for the flight training company on the airport. They had their weapons drawn walking in a slow crouch as they passed though without a word and then they were gone.

"What was that all about?" John asked the guys behind the service desk. They just shrugged their shoulders and one said, "TSA."

Elliot had his scanner and an ear piece as he drove the pick up away from the airport. He knew they were clear because the Homeland Security teams are talking back and forth searching for them.

"How about some hot food?" Elliot asked knowing there would be no complaints. Jerry and Galen answered almost simultaneously, "Yea!"

"I know a great family Italian restaurant on this side of town - it'll be quiet, we can take a break and plan our next move, and they do not have any TVs."

"That sounds great!" Jerry said enthusiastically.

"We should probably try and get some disguises too," Galen suggested, "Our faces are all over the news so if we still want the element of surprise we need to be careful and plan ahead."

They parked behind the restaurant and sat near the back door. The place was almost empty so the food came quickly and the trio ate efficiently and silently.

Elliot stood up and said, "You guys stay here, there's a dollar store next door, I'll pick up some stuff and be back in 15 minutes."

*　　*　　*　　*　　*

Jerry and Galen were in the bathroom putting fake mustaches on. "How does this look?" Jerry asked. "You look like you should be in an 80s porno flick." Galen answered flatly.

"Now this is a great mustache!" Galen announced. They looked at each other, switched mustaches and then both smiled widely.

Elliot threw a Northrup King seed hat and a Bass Pro Shops fishing hat at them. They also grabbed some large sunglasses from the 70s.

They paid for the excellent meal and waved to the cook and they were on their way. Their destination was a nondescript collection of industrial buildings, it looked like a strip mall of industrial buildings.

The sign on the door read 'Smith and Associates.' On one side was a drywall company and on the other a carpet cleaning and snow plowing business. A symmetrical row of tiny ball shaped shrubs was planted between the identical doors.

A Flying Adventure

They drove by slowly and all three in the pickup had their heads turned to follow the front door. Traffic was very light because it was Sunday. Just one car entered the building parking lot – a black Lexus with tinted windows pulled up to the building and parked in a reserved parking spot.

There were 4 visible satellite dishes on the roof and maybe more. This was the only unit with an emergency generator on the roof.

Then they drove by the back side – a row of garage doors. Elliot counted the cameras, "Twenty three" he said.

"What?" said Galen. As they drove out of the area Elliot replied, "I counted 23 cameras all around the building."

"The FBI has been watching this operation for a couple years – we did not get a lot of information on the inside," Elliot explained.

Elliot parked about a block away in another building's parking lot. He passed out radios and ear pieces. He opened another bag and took out a blonde wig and clear glasses. He also put another home made electronic gadget in a back pack along with three small black disks the size of poker chips.

He put on a fake scraggly beard which looked perfect on him. He grabbed a well worn hooded sweatshirt, his backpack, a large manila envelope and a pen.

"I'm going in to gather evidence – if I get in trouble make a diversion," Elliot said seriously. Galen and Jerry looked at each other with a questioning look on their faces.

Elliot put on his hat and walked to the first business in the complex. He entered and asked, "Hi, my name is Jason Bush, are there any job openings?" There were six different buildings in this complex and he went to each one in series.

He even filled out application forms at two of the companies with made up information.

When he got to the carpet cleaning company right next door he asked again if there were any openings.
"It's Sunday!? Come back tomorrow when we're open."

"I work all week, this is the only time I can look for work, I work as a roofer and I gotta find a better job," Elliot pleaded.

The young woman at the desk by the door said there were no openings so Elliot upped his story claiming he had carpet cleaning experience and asked again if he could at least fill out an application.

There was no blank application at her desk so she went to the back room to look for one. Elliot quickly sat down and while shielding himself from the camera removed the electronic device from his back pack, placed it on the floor behind a chair and plugged it in to a wall outlet. It was a small dark brown box, inside were pieces from an old microwave oven, wireless modem, remote control servos and an antenna. Elliot had designed and built the device but this was the first opportunity to use it in the field.

The unit causes video cameras to get very fuzzy. It didn't prevent the camera from sending images; it just makes the images snowy. Elliot surmised that if the cameras went dark, immediate action would be ordered. If the camera was just fuzzy, they would notice but not send a repair tech immediately. He could turn it on and off remotely so he started the deception as soon as he left turning it on and off randomly.

He also stuck one of the self adhesive disks under the edge of the desk. The disks were audio sending devices so he could listen to the sounds inside the offices.

When the young woman came back with an application, he filled it out, thanked her and exited. The next stop was Smith and Associates.

Right inside the door was an entry way that had bullet proof glass – similar to the entrances to jewelry stores. He was startled when the exterior door locked behind him and he found himself looking through the glass into the office and talking on an intercom system to a pair of guards at the reception desk.

"Yea, I am Jason Bush and I am looking for work. Any openings?" Elliot said to the intercom.

"No, it's Sunday, thanks for coming in, good bye," the guards said and the exterior electric door lock clicked open.

"I was wondering if I could at least fill out an application, I need to document my job search for my unemployment, come on guys can you just ask if there are any openings?" Elliot pleaded.

The two guards looked at each other, exchanged a few words but Elliot could not hear them.

The next level of security inside was a tall counter, a metal detector like airports screeners use and the two armed guards wearing bullet proof vests and more cameras.

The door lock into the building buzzed, and Elliot smiled, entered and prepared to fill out the application. He flipped the switch on the video interference machine in the office next door. He wanted to watch them react — he did not see anything but heard shouts and then quiet so he turned it off.

The guards pointed at a biometric hand print scanner on Elliot's side of the wall, "Put your right hand in the scanner and then we'll give you an application."

Uh oh, Elliot could not assume they do not have the FBI or military fingerprint database so he could not put his hand in the scanner.

"Whoa, friends, I got a history that may be a problem and your scanner will see it in a second." Elliot said apologetically. He put one of the disks under the scanner and switched the camera interference on and off.

"I can keep looking, thanks guys," Elliot said as he backed out. The two guards were laughing now.
They buzzed the two doors open and Elliot backed out.

Elliot had a little smirk on his face as he went to the drywall company next door and asked for a job. He continued his charade all the way down to the last company in the complex, stopping at the places that were open. Then, satisfied, he went back to the truck.

Now he would watch and wait and check in with the FBI Deputy Director.

Chapter 53
Salt Lake City, Utah

Madame Leader went to church in the morning and back to work in the afternoon. As she drove into her building's parking lot in her black Lexus she saw a trio of men that looked like the product of an incestual union. She wishes she could live in a pure Mormon state. Utah still had too many non-believers.

She was in too good a mood to be much affected by these idiots who lived in the same city, same state, and same country as her. Luckily no one had parked in her parking spot.

She greeted the guards, rushed past them and briskly walked directly to her office and began reviewing video.   She had stringers across the country that fed her interesting video from parking lot cameras, hotel lobby cameras, traffic cameras and other public cameras. She was amazed that people could be so stupid – the things they did in public! She also has cameras in official church vehicles and some Homeland Security and TSA vehicles.

Her office was in the center of the building, three walls had 72 inch high definition televisions. The fourth wall was a clear glass wall with a glass door. There were no windows and recessed lights and built in glowing accent pieces on the walls. She had an electric shade on the window wall for privacy. Her desk was semicircular and has a video editing station built into it. There were no chairs other than her own in office—everyone stands, except her.

She was a quick learner and an astute reader of people. She could identify people who could be manipulated and could tell when people are lying.

Sunday afternoon was an easy work day – not many people in the office. She had a couple of calls to make and then she could relax.

She dialed a number in Washington DC.

"Hello this is Stuart."

"Stuart, darling, this is your old new friend," Madam Leader said in her most seductive voice. "Have you had a chance to reconsider?"

"Yes, I have considered your offer and I have to tell you that you are out of your league. You simply do not know who you are dealing with," Stuart replied confidently.

"Really? Well you go right ahead, I can simply send my information anonymously to your agency's Internal Affairs office and your career is over, your trophy wife is gone, your kids will forget about you as you busy yourself in prison fighting off boyfriends," she said with out missing a beat.

"I can handle that, obviously you do not know what I went through to get this position and the friends I made on the way," Stuart said stubbornly.

"Right, you can handle it," she said sarcastically. "But what about your kids and your wife?" She paused for effect and whispered, "And you think the worst I can do is blackmail?"

"You are more valuable to me alive but you are only slightly less valuable to me dead!" another pause for an even deeper effect.

"I can use your death as an example to the others… so, your choice, either play along like a good boy or help me convince others that I am serious…you have 15 seconds." Madam leader's voice was cold.

After 15 seconds she said, "OK, thanks for playing along, I will have a parting gift for you in the green room."

"Ok, I understand, what do you want?" Stuart said desperately.

"I just want some information once in a while," she said sweetly. "I would like more information about your agency's internal affairs – I need you to send me some names, addresses and phone numbers of that division," she asked innocently.

"If I do that, is that all?" he asked.

"Of course, Stuart, you can trust me," she said

Stuart was ready to negotiate but Madam Leader had disconnected her call and Stuart was left, heart beating and sweat beading. He had been trying to find out something on his blackmailer but he had nothing yet. He was Chief of Staff for the Vice Secretary of Homeland Security. He could influence but he could not do anything – anything that would be valuable to her.

Madam Leader called her next partner. She reviewed his file on her computer. This guy was not a black mail case – she simply bribed him. He would do anything for money. She just facilitated. She helped people get what they want.

"Hello Casey?" Madam Leader asked. Casey never said Hi or hello he just picked up the call and says "Yea"

"Casey, I need another favor, I need you to stall the investigation, do what ever you can – you have a budget to use at your discression," she said.

"Whatever…" he said with a shrug. Madam Leader piped up, "I've transferred $50,000 to your account in the Bahamas – get it done immediately!"

"Hey, is your mission for real? Are the rumors true? Something with the food supply?" Casey asked

"Of course not, this is a conspiracy designed to distract the gullible public – the usual deception used by your government to maintain their power. You are a true patriot, thank you Casey." Madam Leader said in an encouraging tone.

She was having a productive day but she was getting annoyed that there hadn't been illnesses reported from the altered milk. Another crisis would allow the mess in South Dakota to burn out and die down. Give the media something else to look at and in a week everyone would forget about it.

Chapter 54
Salt Lake City, Utah

E lliot attached his satellite phone to the receiver for the audio microphones in the building housing Smith and Associates. He listened while they waited for darkness before making their move.

Jerry lay in the back of the pickup, taking a nap while Galen studied the equipment and the building while listening in with Elliot.

He was excited and getting energized planning and was now actually looking forward to their mission. Elliot dug in his bag and said, "Galen, you gotta see this!" as he pulled out another handheld unit with a disk shaped antenna on top. "I borrowed this from the Secret Service," he said, holding up two fingers in each hand and making those quote signs when he said 'borrowed'.

"OK, I give up, what does it do?" Galen asked in a playful manner. "This is a cell phone jammer, they use it when they are protecting the President!" Elliot explained.

"That's cool, but won't it jam our communication too?" Galen asked. Elliot reassured him, "It can be adjusted so that one frequency can be allowed to work."

"Here is what I am most proud of – this is an audio and video interceptor and sender. I just use these sensors here and clamp on to the cables and it reformats the signal and sends it to this satellite phone and on to the FBI."

Galen was speechless – he had never seen such equipment. "I was losing some confidence because this mission is kinda '3 against an army' but I believe this will work. What do I do?"

"After midnight, you come with me, Jerry will stay here and watch the equipment," Elliot explained. "We need to enter through the drywall company, I've checked it out. We set up the gear and then confront her when she gets in."

Galen's phone rang, he looked at the number and his eyes got wide. He jerked away from Elliot and walked while answering,

"Hello?"

"Galen my dear friend, what news have you for me?" He recognized Her voice, "Oh, it's you, your voice sounded almost human."

"You are such a talented man, police chief, comedian, husband…, well, widower. Enough pleasantries, what is the status of your adventure?"

"We are at a little airport in Medicine Bow Wyoming, the plane broke down, something about a broken wheel. It's cold and we're hungry, what more can I tell you?" Galen answered sullenly.

"What are your plans?" She asked quickly.

"We're grounded, Jerry is looking for a junked wheel to put on the plane, no one here has identified us so far," Galen answered.

"Thank you so much Galen, I know I can trust you, and you can trust me."

"Remember you were going to fix it so I am cleared—maybe you could make it look like I am bringing Jerry in."

"We'll see," Madam Leader bluffed—she had no intention of doing anything to help Galen. She hung up the phone.

Galen had walked a half block away from the truck and his partners. He returned with a story about a call from the Pierre Police Department.

When he returned he caught part of a conversation between Elliot and the FBI.

Elliot said, "We are right on target, are you receiving from our transmitters?"

The Deputy Director was pleased, "Yes, it's working great." Elliot noticed Galen walk back and he waved for him to come closer.
"Are you certain your science experiments will work?" The Deputy Director asked.
"It'll work; I hope we can get everyone associated with this conspiracy," Elliot answered positively.

The Deputy Director urgently insisted, "We gotta get this tomorrow because we can't deceive Her much longer—by Monday morning the crisis should be all over the news, when it is not, she will know something is wrong and will go into her shell."

Elliot quickly replied, "We gotta get this right while she has her guard down."

"We'll keep monitoring your transmissions and have a team ready when you need them," the Deputy Director said as he ended the call. "Good luck and be safe."

Chapter 55
Sioux Falls, South Dakota

With every minute flying away from Broken Bow Nebraska to Springfield, Minnesota, Lynn Sherwood and the two girls relaxed a bit more. The Piper Warrior had been flying perfectly. Moderate fuel burn, light winds, and the weather was quite smooth. She estimated they will be in Springfield in about another hour.

Jerry suggested she not use the communication radio and transponder and that was not a problem. On this Sunday afternoon they did not even see another plane. The winds were light and there were few thermals so the ride was wonderful as they flew over rich farmland and successful farmsteads. You could tell they are successful by counting the number of shiny new galvanized steel grain bins. These sparkling structures were visible miles away.

She left after talking with Jerry and agreed not to use her cell phone or credit cards. She plotted a course to Springfield which would take them within 30 miles of Sioux Falls, South Dakota.

She monitored the engine instruments and listened in to the Sioux Falls airport tower. Listening to traffic calls and pilot reports on the radio passes time. She imagines their day—flying for fun or business and she tried to identify the aircraft from the pilots call.

The girls kept talking about the swimming pool at the place they would stay tonight. How big the pool would be, whether it would have a slide or even a hot tub. Lynn said, "I said a dozen times already, I am not certain we will have a pool." They said, "But most motels have a pool don't they?"

"Mommy!, Mommy!, Mommy!" they said. "Look at that," they said pointing out the side window.

An F-16 fighter jet was flying alongside of the plane at the same altitude – it was close, so close she could see the pilot in his helmet and tinted visor. Seconds later Lynn noticed another F-16 fighter on the other side of the plane. When she made eye contact the pilot pointed to the ground. She looked at the other plane and that pilot pointed at her and then pointed to the ground.

The jets were flying with full flaps and landing gear down and as slow as they could with their nose high trying to stay with the slower Piper single engine propeller plane.

Lynn knew the adventure was over, she turned the plane towards the Sioux Falls airport and made her call to the tower. She was given a straight in approach and landing. The two jets escorted her and as she touched down, they accelerated and climbed almost straight up and around and landed behind her.

She was instructed to taxi to the ramp away from the terminal. Police cars and airport security trucks circled the plane, the officers got out and aimed their weapons at the plane and ordered them out.

Lynn yelled out the half opened door, "I want the FBI, not TSA or Homeland Security!" The officers yelled for everyone to get out right now, no one would get hurt. Lynn relaxed and could see there were no TSA or Homeland Security officers. She opened the door and held the kid's hands as they exited. She and the girls walked away but the officers kept their weapons aimed at the plane.

196

A Flying Adventure

Lynn was confused. The lead officer yelled at the plane, "Get out of the plane, give yourself up, there is no way to escape!" Lynn and the girls looked at each other with puzzled looks on their faces. Finally the officers talked to Lynn, "Where is Jerry? Where is the dirty bomb?"

Lynn shook her head and yelled at the officers, "There is no one in the plane and there is no dirty bomb, we are just on our way to Springfield, Minnesota, to a hotel with a pool!" The kids started yelling, "Yea, we are going to have a pool!"

The armed men approached the plane and inspected every part. Lynn wanted to leave but was taken to the police station. She asked for an attorney and she finally felt safe as long as she could stay away from any Transportation Security Agency and Homeland Security officers.

Chapter 56
Pierre, South Dakota

Beano and the Homeland Security Leader finally realized they were on the same side. The Homeland Security Field Leader mentioned some of his concern about his commanders.

"What would it hurt if you made an anonymous report to your Internal Affairs team to look into the orders?" Beano asked sincerely.

"We are making real progress on what happened here," Beano continued. "Those men were wrong to kidnap Lynn Sherwood but they were then murdered by someone. We need to find out who is behind this."

The Homeland Security Field Commander agreed, "We have conflicting information about the leader of the conspiracy, we have the bacteria from the failed sabotage but the perpetrators must have had some help getting away."

"Our investigation found threads of evidence leading back to shell corporations, holding companies and dead ends. What concerns me most is the false information, deception, lack of cooperation and outright obfuscation from your agency, Homeland Security and to a lesser degree TSA," Beano said with authority.

"Wow Beano, obfuscation, pretty fancy word from a South Dakota boy!" the Homeland Security commander chided with a smile.

"Awh shucks, ain't no big thing – we are on the same side buddy!" Beano's big grin returned.

Chapter 57
Washington DC

Project Hotel Sierra, the group that watched Homeland Security, was reporting to the Deputy Director in the personal conference room of the FBI Director. The room was huge, with leather conference chairs, a horseshoe shaped table with built in monitors and a gigantic video screen the size of some football stadium scoreboards.

Included in the conference were the members of the Executive Leadership team -- everyone except the Director himself.

"This whole operation began with a group of TSA subcontractors assisting Joseph Smith, a former Marine, in bringing a genetically engineered strain of bacteria from the Philippines to Canada into the US via Pierre, South Dakota. Jerry Sherwood killed Joe Smith and was then smeared by Homeland Security. Galen Anderson was smeared in the same kind of media blitz when he got too close to the truth," the Project Manager solemnly reported.

"The trucks and the subcontractors can be directly connected to TSA and Homeland Security and we have strong evidence they coordinated the flights or allowed them to happen. They helped distribute the bacteria. The funding has not been traceable ...yet," added the unit Manager.

The Deputy Director stood and began, "We have been watching a secret leadership organization inside the Mormon church for about a year. Recently we were able to set up one of our employees to be blackmailed by the leader of that secret group. We have an operation that is gathering information on the group right now."

The Project Manager finished his part of the presentation, "We have strong evidence that many leaders in Homeland Security have been compromised, either through blackmail or simply paid off and we are executing arrest warrants tonight!"

The unit manager explained further, "We must strike today against that leadership group in the Church of Latter Day Saints – up to this point they think their plan to poison the drinkable milk supply has been successful."

The Deputy Director interrupted, "We believe the motivation is two fold, they want to destabilize the economy which will drive more funding and more power to Homeland Security and then to the Leadership of the Mormon Church. We also believe this is industrial sabotage since many of the milk plants not attacked were owned by the Mormon Church."

"We consider this an 'All hands on Deck' moment: we need all resources focused on this project. The project manager will be coordinating efforts for the next couple of days," said the Deputy Director as the unit manager was handed out the task list.

"In conclusion I want to thank every one of you for working this weekend, your efforts are recognized and appreciated." said the Deputy Director as he closed his portfolio. "Thank you."

Chapter 58
Salt Lake City, Utah

J
erry woke up and groaned, "What's the plan, what's our status?" Galen and Elliot monitored the listening devices while assembling their gear.

"Jerry, you're staying in the truck tonight, to monitor the gear and watch our backs. We need you to be ready to call the cavalry." Elliot tried to soften the blow. Jerry expected to go with him.

Jerry had a hurt look on his face when he said, "Hey guys, we need to finish this and I can help!"

"Look, Jerry, you've been through a lot but this is too dangerous and this is simply not for you." Galen was trying to bring Jerry down gently.

Jerry got out of the truck and said, "I'm going for a walk to get some snacks." He gave them his best 'You guys are making a big mistake' face and walked to a convenience store a couple of blocks away.

He was angry and walked with quick, firm steps pushing into the ground as he muttered to himself. When he got to the store he bought soft drinks, protein bars, oranges and bananas. He had an armful of stuff as he waited in line; in front of him stood a pretty young woman in a plain wool dress coat and skirt. She was buying a coffee and some breath mints. As she left she noticed Jerry and looked into his eyes as if she recognized him. Jerry was surprised until he remembered he was all over the news, his face was on the cover of the newspapers at the check out counter.

He was still wearing the mustache and seed hat but maybe she recognized him. He quickly turned away and walked to pick up a Ding Dong.

She gathered her stuff, looked at the newspapers then looked at Jerry again and slowly walked out the store to her car. She drove to Joseph Smith and Associates and entered. The Security Guards welcomed her as she went through the metal detector. She went straight for her Mothers' office.

"Mom, what have you heard from your contact about the Pierre Police Chief and Jerry Sherwood?" Mary Rose asked Madam Leader who was shuffling her files.

"They are grounded at an airport in Wyoming, we can clean them up later – they are not a factor to the immediate plan," she replied without even looking up from her monitor.

"OK, good, how about his wife, is she still available?" Mary Rose asked sneaking a peak at her mother's gigantic work station. "She could be nice leverage."

"Well, you better get on that, instead of standing here watching me work," Madam Leader barked. "Why are you here, you should be at home making grandchildren," she yelled over her shoulder as Mary Rose left the office.

Mary Rose trudged to her own office, a small, plain office with grey furniture. She immediately started monitoring the digital files from cameras around the building for the day. She watched them in fast forward to see what she needed to see.

She saw an odd looking man cold calling on the businesses in the building complex, on a Sunday afternoon. She went back further and saw a pickup with 3 odd looking men drive slowly by the front and back of the building.

She subtly emptied out her desk of any personal information and put the stuff in a plastic bag. She also transferred files from the mainframe to her portable computer. She quietly copied contact lists, account numbers and passwords of the accounts to which she had access.

Mary Rose checked the live feed from the exterior cameras looking for anything out of order. She spent the next couple of hours calling her network – the women's network was a strong, secret network of Mormon women who supported each other and guided the church in the direction they believed the church needed to go. She was calling to confirm the numbers were still accurate and that network would be available for a potential project.

Chapter 59
Salt Lake City, Utah

Elliot Ray, Galen Anderson and Jerry Sherwood sat silently in the borrowed pick up truck waiting for dark and the opportunity to protect the country. They were parked across the street about half a block away. They could see most of the building through trees and shrubs.

Jerry slept at dusk and Galen tried to take a nap, closed his eyes and then woke to look around. He was restless and anxious. Elliot called his boss and confirmed there would be a SWAT team ready to go in the morning and that the local FBI did not know about this operation.

Elliot and Galen held their weapons out of sight to clean and attached silencers. Elliot had a big backpack filled with electronic gizmos. Galen's bag was filled with percussive grenades, tie wraps, duct tape, portable timed explosives, rope and extra ammunition.

"We go in at about 1:00 AM so relax until then." Elliot watched employees leave and lights get turned off after cleaning crews completed cleaning each office.

*   *   *   *   *   *

There were between 15 and 20 guards at all times in the Operations Building. Five guards at a time monitor about 50 cameras at 11 different locations around Salt Lake City. They monitored cameras at churches, schools, the Administrative building and the Apostles' and Prophets' houses. They rotate every two hours so that fresh eyes are always watching and computers were recording everything. There were also several crews of guards on patrol at all times.

"There it goes again," one of the monitoring guards said.
"Yeah, those cameras over there have been kinda intermittent. I saw a note that a maintenance order has already been completed—the technician will be here in the morning," the other guard said.

"I just have never seen anything like that—it is snowy and hard to identify if anything is going on over there."
"It's not such a big deal, it's next door, and that doesn't really affect us here anyway."

The first guard finally reached out and tapped the monitors that were fuzzy. The second guard watched and wondered, "Why do humans tap a nonfunctioning electronic object as if their fingers were magic and their gentle tapping will have any effect of the operation?"

*   *   *   *   *

Elliot and Galen walked up to the building and directly to the door of the office next door. He turned on the remote switch that caused the video cameras to send snowy - fuzzy images. Elliot used his lock picking skills and opened the door in seconds. He went directly to the alarm system and attached an electronic box with LED lights over the alarm control box. The alarm was disarmed in seconds and they were free to move around the office.

They both moved into a storage room that shared a wall with Joseph Smith and Associates. Elliot and Galen moved tables and shelves so they could climb up and into the ceiling. The building was constructed of cement block walls and a flat roof supported by steel trusses. Elliot expected the builders did not make the walls go to the roof. He guessed that the Mormons would believe that since their video surveillance was so good additional security would not be needed.

Once outside the view of the cameras, he turned off the remote control on the video jammer. They climbed up through the ceiling into the space between the ceiling and the steel corrugated roof. They had to crawl between the steel rods of the trusses and there was a large problem. Galen could not climb between the truss parts. These trusses were built with 2 angle iron pieces on top and 2 on the bottom with steel rod welded in a W pattern the entire length of the span.

"Jerry, we have a problem," whispered Elliot into the radio ear pieces they all were wearing. "Galen is too big around the middle to squeeze between the bars on the trusses." He would not be able to accompany Elliot.

"Galen will let you in, we need you right away."

Jerry was nervous but excited and Galen was very disappointed.

"I gotta eat better food," he said under his breath.

Galen reluctantly went back to the truck to monitor the transmissions and Jerry grabbed the back pack and followed Elliot through the trusses into the area above Smith and Associates.

Elliot used hand signals to guide Jerry and they had to move very slowly so they would make no noise. Even whispering might be noticed now. Elliot read the wiring like a road map. He could see the junction boxes and the satellite feeds. He needed to get to the main output of the monitoring center and hook up his new parasite electronic device.

He pulled the device out of his backpack. He had used parts from cell phones, handmade sensors put into a solid aluminum camera case. This was hooked up to his second satellite phone. The apparatus was designed to intercept the video feed without interrupting them and send them on to the FBI headquarters.

"Galen, it this working, are you seeing the feed?" Elliot whispered.

"Yes, it is working." He was watching a tiny 2 inch monitor and switching between the different views.

They said as little as possible and worked quietly. Jerry was struggling just to keep up with Elliot, who was working quickly and silently. Elliot was looking for Madam Leader's office – they would drop into her office and wait for her there.

Elliot found the office and an access door in the wooden ceiling. He had to disassemble the locking mechanism to get it to open. Before he opened it he removed another video jammer and turned it on. They could hear the guards in the monitoring room talking.

"There goes some more cameras – look here," The guard said while pointing to the snowy monitors.

"OK, let's write this up like the others"
"Shouldn't we check it out?"
"Na, everything looks good."

Elliot and Jerry dropped into the Leaders office and slid under her huge semicircular desk to regroup. After they are situated and quiet, Elliot made the fuzzy video clear again.

They relaxed and simply waited for Madam Leader to show up.

Chapter 60
6:30 AM, Salt Lake City, Utah

In a school parking lot about 6 blocks from Smith and Associates the FBI Special Weapons and Tactics Team assembled. There was barely enough light to see each other and dawn was about 15 minutes away.

"Let's do a short review, we'll wait for the word. The straight truck will go first and then about 2 minutes later the armored personnel carrier. The helicopter will be hovering, to monitor and synchronize with the other groups," the Commander said.

"There will be between 15 and 20 guards throughout the building, there will also be about 30 to 40 women employees. The guards are armed, expect severe resistance. Deadly force is authorized with the guards. We want all the employees so we will have the locals set up a perimeter and secure the site."

"They are known to set booby traps so keep your eyes open. One more thing, we will have two agents inside, don't shoot them!"

*　　*　　*　　*　　*

Mary Rose went to the convenience store, for her usual coffee and parked a half block away from Smith and Associates. The dawn sky was colorful. Blues and purple changed to red and orange. She parked on the other side of the building away from Galen and the pickup with the communication equipment. She arrived earlier than normal – she knew something was happening today and she wanted a good view of the action.

Employees were entering the building for work randomly and within 15 minutes Madam Leader drove up. Mary Rose ducked down in her seat and peeked out. Her mother did not recognize her daughter's car as she parked in her designated parking spot and went in.

*   *   *   *   ·   *

Galen tried to sleep but now that dawn was upon them, he perked up. He found some leftover juice and one of the Ding Dongs. "I gotta start eating better food" he said to himself. He ducked down when he saw Madam Leader drive up. Galen was preparing to enter the building with the SWAT team—he liked the action—he didn't come all this way to not get in on the excitement.

"Elliot, Jerry; she is here and on her way in."

"Acknowledged," whispered Elliot into the radio transmitter in his ear.

Inside, Madam Leader quickly brushed by the guards at the door. Her assistants were ready and waiting to hand her updated reports and files. She accepted the files and was reviewed them as she walked into her office. She tossed the reports onto the desk and they slid across the spotless surface. She walked around and sat down in her chair and pulled herself up to the desk.

Elliot and Jerry were hidden under the large desk. Elliot gripped his hand gun tightly, feeling the weight of the weapon and silencer. He gave the signal to Jerry and together they made their move.

Elliot slid the pistol between her legs under her dress; she screamed and Jerry grabbed her chair and pulled it close.

"Don't move and don't scream and you may live." He whispered loudly.

"What? Who are you?"

Elliot whispered to Jerry, "Put the zip ties on her arms and legs." Jerry strapped her ankles to the casters and her wrists to the arms of the executive chair.

"You guys are the stupidest guys on the face of the earth – you will never get away with this."

"Get away with this, ha, the mission is already accomplished. This was always a suicide mission!"

Jerry whipped his head around and with mouth open he stared wide eyed at Elliot. Elliot rolled his eyes and then winked.

"You guys are morons, I have an army of well trained and armed guards who will kill you and dispose of your bodies in an acid bath and flush your remains down the toilet."

"You've never been shot before have you," Elliot said softly. "The bullet burns like a red hot cast iron poker and the pain makes you lose focus and then parts of your body don't work right."

"Who do you work for? Someone in the church? CIA, FBI, the Mafia?"

"Are you really that ignorant," Elliot asked.

Then Jerry said, "Look, you nasty old lady, we know a lot about you and we caught you – now, how does that feel?"

"She's delusional." Elliot teased.

"Who are you guys?" She had a smile on her face. She was thinking of her options as she was talking. Soon her assistants would be coming in.

"Close the curtain and lock the door – I know you have a remote, so do it!"

Madam Leader hesitated and Elliot shoved the gun and silencer a little further.

"Oh, Ooh, Ah, you have wonderful skills," She cooed as she rocked her hips against the barrel of the weapon. She was trying to manipulate them but Elliot and Jerry were not being affected.

"Umpf, here's how it's going to happen. I pull the trigger and the bullet rips through your lower abdomen and smashes through your spine and exits into the wall behind you in a fountain of blood."

"The pain will make you scream out, but it's already too late. In 30 seconds enough blood will have left your body that you will feel no pain. You will hallucinate and feel bathed in a warm glow and in another 30 seconds, you will be dead."

She was shaken, and for about 15 seconds she was scared. Then she thought a bit and her confidence came back.
"Screw you, you don't have the guts to pull the trigger." She was seething. "You probably have never even killed anyone."

Jerry spoke up, "You don't know…" Elliot quickly hit him to get him to shut up and keep quiet.

"What? He speaks!" She sarcastically remarked at Jerry's outburst. She was working the two of them, trying to get them to make a mistake.

A Flying Adventure

"Listen you scheming vermin, we know your game, we know your plan, we know your weakness." Jerry had said too much. Elliot was happy, Jerry performed right on cue.

She rolled a little bit back trying to get a look at his face. She recognized his face.
"Jerry Sherwood? Is that you? Oh how rich! How precious. You're here to get revenge? You are not worth my time."

"Don't say anything Jerry, let me handle this."

"Is that Galen, no, it must be Elliot, Galen is out there betraying you. He has been my operative for months."

"*I have not betrayed you, I'm still in the truck, everything is going right on plan.*" Galen replied through the radio receivers in their ears.

"Now I'm going to tell you how it is going to go. You are going to release my feet and hands and give me your weapons and I will turn you over to the police and you may even live." Madam Leader lowered her voice for the last phrase and controlled her anger barely.

Elliot tilted the weapon down and fired a shot; the bullet went through her dress and out the chair seat bottom. Madam Leader jumped and then as Elliot immediately touched the hot gun barrel to her thigh, she shrieked. The slug hit the floor and ricocheted to the wall with a loud thud.

Elliot also switched on the fuzzy video jammer.
Her phone rang; she could see it was from her Security Consol operators.
"Answer it." Elliot said as he cut the zip tie on her left hand. "And no funny business."
"Yes?" she said as she answered the call.

213

"Excuse me Madam Leader, we heard a loud noise and wanted to make sure everything is OK."

"I'm fine; I dropped a book, Thanks for your concern." She hung up the phone and Jerry strapped her hand back to the arm of the chair and Elliot turned off the fuzzy video.

"Are you guys OK, do you need anything?" Galen asked through their ear receivers.

"So what do you want?" She asked

Jerry spoke. "We want you to clear our names, Galen and me, and we want you to release Elliot's parents."

Then Elliot interrupted again. "She probably doesn't have that much power, she doesn't control that much. I think she did it and that's enough for me."

"Wait Elliot, remember what we are here for" Jerry said.

"You guys disgust me, all talk and no action. You don't know who you are dealing with. You don't have a plan and you are wasting my time."

"With a word I can take out you and your families and that's exactly what will happen if you kill me"

"You've seen the result of my orders. You and others like you are expendable, just toy soldiers on a playing field. I ordered the trucks outfitted with cameras and explosives and I flipped the switch to protect the church and our future."

"I believe you can do the media smear but you don't have the commitment to murder someone, or as you say, multiple murders." Elliot said giving another wink and nod to Jerry.

"Oh yes, I have the power and the vision to see the future and I am disciplined enough to make sacrifices to get us where we need to be."

"Those trucks are not the only vehicles with explosives and remote controls."

Elliot was tempted to ask more questions but he stayed to the plan.

"And the bacteria, what's the plan with that?" Elliot asked.

"It's too late for you, my little friend with the big gun. The bacteria has been delivered and now we just wait for the chaos. Congress and the President will demand more power and funding for Homeland Security because of the failings of the FBI and CIA." Madam Leader said with a laugh.

"The church is bigger than you or me and your agencies – we will survive and thrive and ultimately we will prevail. You can't stop me and you can't stop us"

"Home Land Security is mine because I control the leaders. When they get lots of money and power, I get lots of power."

"I squash people like you. I will enjoy killing you. I' only telling you this because there is no chance you will make it out of here alive."

"I can see the SWAT team coming—you have 15 seconds before all hell breaks out." Galen announced.

"Jerry, remove the zip ties."

They heard a huge boom, the lights flickered, another large explosion, then multiple percussion grenades. From the office they heard men shouting and women screaming.

The armored personnel carrier flew down the street and squealed the tires as it turned into the parking lot and drove directly into the reception area of Smith and Associates. The men inside were bounced around a bit when the 6 wheel vehicle with the 300 horsepower v-10 engine slammed through the walls and glass doors. The two men at the reception desk were crushed and killed instantly. The vehicle drove all the way into the office, filling it completely. The men poured out of the personnel carrier taking heavy fire and began firing their weapons at the guards carrying weapons.

The SWAT team took positions and yelled at the women, "Remain on the floor and you will not be killed!"

The guards paused for a second and then resumed shooting. The bullets where pinging off the personnel carrier. The guards were dropping and only two SWAT Team members were hit. They were wearing body armor and were well trained in urban tactics and excellent at firearms.

Galen ran in with his shotgun after the SWAT team and started firing at the guards.

The second very large explosion was from the men in the truck that backed up to the reinforced loading dock doors. Twenty men streamed into the offices, working from room to room. The guards were all ready to continue the fire fight, they thought they had superior numbers but they were wrong.

A few of the guards surrendered and fell on the ground as the SWAT team members secured the surrendering guards with zip ties and then started taking custody of the women who work there.

In Madam Leader's office the lights went out with the second explosion. Jerry and Elliot turned on LED lights attached to their hats and tackled Madam Leader to protect her from the explosions and control her. Her hands were free as Jerry was cutting the zip ties to her ankles. Elliot had his weapon on her from a safe distance.

After Galen warned Jerry and Elliot he found the bullet proof vest with big letters POLICE on the back. He ran for the opening made by the armored personnel carrier while pulling on the vest and juggling the shotgun. Galen found Madam Leaders office, tried the door, and fired a shotgun blast at the lock. The glass in the door shattered but it didn't open.

When Galen shot the door lock, the noise startled Elliot and Jerry and they turned to the door. Madam leader escaped briefly, dived towards her desk, opened a drawer grabbed her weapon and fired blindly at the door. Elliot and Jerry tackled her and she fired again. Elliot smashed her in the face and grabbed her arms while Jerry held her legs. They had her under control so Jerry aimed his headlight towards the door and saw Galen slumped through the door halfway into the room.

He yelled out, "Galen!" He let Elliot finish securing Madam Leader and ran to Galen and pulled him free of the door. A bullet had missed the body armor hitting him in the neck. Blood was pouring out of the wound. Jerry put his hand over the gash and pressed hard. Galen winched and moaned.
"You'll be OK, the ambulance is right outside—they'll be in when the place is secure, Galen, can you hear me?"

Galen looked at Jerry with a weak smile. He tried to talk but nothing came out. Jerry looked at the pool of blood and Galen's blood soaked clothes, wondering how much blood Galen had already lost. He searched urgently for the EMT's.
"Galen, we did it, we got the evidence, and you heard everything right? Our names are cleared!"

Elliot was dragging Madam Leader towards the door. Jerry looked helplessly up at Elliot. Galen was fading, he was limp and struggled to keep his eyes open.

"You'll be OK Galen, I got your back. This was quite an adventure." Galen opened his eyes a bit and smiled thinly.

"Yea, we had some great adventures, lots of stories to tell." Jerry said. "I am glad to know you."

Galen's breathing slowed, became shallower and ended with a sigh as he died.

Chapter 61
FBI Headquarters, Washington DC

T he Deputy Director was in the Command Center monitoring the audio and video feeds from the Leadership Council headquarters in Salt Lake City.

"Wow, this is excellent, can we really see all of their video?"

"We can see everything they can see, would you like to scan some of the other cameras?" the audio and video technician asked.

"No, this is excellent; make sure we have copies of everything. Get me the SWAT Commander."

Another Communication Specialist arranged the call,
"It's ready Sir."
"Commander, what's your status?"
"Ready. We are about a half mile from the target and ready to go."
"Stand by, any second, we are monitoring the feed and we will send you in when we have the evidence."

Everyone in the control room was listening intently and watching the Deputy Director. When Madam Leader admitted to the bacteria terrorism and the murders they received the green light.

"Commander, go, Go, GO!"

Chapter 62
Salt Lake City, Utah

Mary Rose was watching the Smith and Associates building from her car about a half block away. She had her favorite flavored coffee and a magazine to read while she waited. About 15 minutes after her mother entered the building she heard the commotion before she saw it.

An armored troop carrier roared down the street, black smoke pouring out of its exhaust pipe. It turned into the parking lot going too fast. It jumped a curb and slammed through the entry of the office. She sat up in the car and made an audible gasp. Police cars, ambulances and unmarked police cars followed and setting up around the building, sealing the area.

She jumped in her seat when she heard explosions and gunfire. She started the car and gripped the wheel ready to peel out but she had to stay and watch. After about two minutes of solid gunfire, men yelling and women screaming there was finally silence.

She sighed and took a sip of coffee. Mary Rose grasped a small padded envelope holding a flash drive. She put latex gloves on and wiped the envelope and flash drive clean with an alcohol swab. On the flash drive was video of her mother admitting she ordered the bacterial attack. It was addressed to FBI Field Office Manager Elliot Ray. As the ambulances rolled closer and the EMT's were waved in, Mary Rose dialed a number on her cell phone.

"It's done, time to go to plan B. I am on my way."

Chapter 63
Salt Lake City, Utah

T he Emergency Medical Technicians scrambled around Galen and guided Jerry away while they worked on him. Within a couple of minutes they looked up to Jerry and simply shook their heads. They had used the defibrillator, given him intravenous fluid and patched the gunshot wound but there was so much blood loss, so quickly, the outcome was terminal.

Elliot walked Madam Leader to what was once the front door, they had to walk over concrete blocks, steel 2 x 4's and drywall and wires. He was not about to turn her over to any stranger. He waited until he saw a familiar face, another FBI agent. Madam Leader would be brought in a separate vehicle to a secure undisclosed location to avoid the possibility of more problems.

All the women employees were brought to the Salt Lake City police station for interrogation and all would be prosecuted using the evidence. Forensic technicians would be working the scene for months. They were lucky Madam Leader was under control when they raided the facility. They found explosives placed around the building wired to remote detonators in Madam Leaders' office. Her office was protected, they theorized she would destroy the building around her, including co-workers and raiders, and escape.

Jerry walked alongside Galen's body as it was wheeled to the ambulance. He remembered the obvious melancholy on Galen's face when he had hugged Lynn. Jerry had been delighted and relieved to have his wife and daughters in his arms, but Galen had no such warm family embrace.

221

He also remembered how noble Galen had looked standing on the highway outside of town at the site of the TSA agents who were killed in the explosion of their truck. He was confident and in charge as he gave instructions to Buck and Lynn and Jerry. A person can seem small and insignificant against the backdrop of the South Dakota prairie.

He smiled as he remembered Galen asleep as they flew. Galen always had a peaceful expression on his face. He would miss Galen, he was absolutely the right person to have as a partner in this adventure. He was good with a gun and had that practical common sense that Jerry appreciated.

As the ambulance drove away Jerry saw Elliot. He waved and they walked towards each other.

"Did we really get the evidence we need to clear our names and put her away?"

"I think we did, we have the evidence and I think this is over."
"What about your Mom and Dad, are they OK?"

"I gotta be honest. I made that up so I could go along with you and Galen. Jerry, listen, we did good today. Most people are good but sometimes we need to sacrifice when we take care of the bad people."
They shook hands.

"You need to get professional counseling after all you have been through," Elliot said seriously.

"I will but right now I gotta call Lynn and see how she is." Jerry told Elliot as he fumbled with his cell phone. He dialed Lynn's number.

"Lynn, it's me, everything is fine. We were successful, mission accomplished."

"Jerry you jerk, taking chances like that," Lynn said.

"Honey, I miss you and I love you. I can't wait to see you again."

"We are leaving for home in a couple of hours, I'll tell you about our adventure."

"Cool. Home. It will be nice to be home. Where is home? Our house is wrecked."

"When we are together, that's home," she said softly.

"I can't wait, but it looks like I gotta go, call me again before you take off, I love you."

"I love you too." Jerry said slowly as he watched the FBI agents gather the women and guards.

He ran to catch up with Elliot.

"Elliot, you must return to Pierre with me to tell the story to Galen's family. They probably won't believe me."
Elliot smiled a tired smile and said, "Sure thing Jerry."

"I'll never forget Galen and you … and what we did together."

"Yea, all in a days work right?"

"By the way, Jerry, what do you do for work?"

"I am glad you asked, because I believe I can help you. What kind of insurance does the FBI provide? Life? Disability? What kind of retirement plan do you have?" Elliot smiled as Jerry continued.

"What you want to do is manage risk. A young guy like you can have an excellent future **if** you plan ahead."

Elliot rolled his eyes and laughed as they walked back to the truck with their belongings and equipment.

"You sell insurance? I should have figured that out." Elliot responded.

"Hey do you want a ride back to Sioux Falls?"
"No, they will keep me busy here for days."
"Don't forget your promise to help me tell Galen's story"
"I won't forget, I'll be there," Elliot replied.

The End

Published by Seitview Publishing

themormonconspiracy@yahoo.com